THE BOY WHO DARED

SUSAN CAMPBELL BARTOLETTI

SCHOLASTIC INC.

ISBN 978-1-338-33533-0

12 11 10 9 8 7 6 5 4 3 2 1   18 19 20 21 22 23

Printed in the U.S.A. 40

Originally published in hardcover by Scholastic Press, February 2008

This edition first printing, September 2018

Book design by Phil Falco
The text type was set in Palatino.

Special thanks to Hermann Teifer, archivist at the Leo Baeck Institute,
for his expert fact-checking of the manuscript. Thanks also to National
Holocaust Museum docent William Werner Hess and to LDS Church
members Tim Wadham and Nadine Hubbard for their invaluable
consultations. And to Carole Hess of Nürnberg, Germany,
for translating the notice on page 185.

FOR JOE

DEATH ROW
PLÖTZENSEE PRISON
BERLIN, GERMANY

OCTOBER 27, 1942

DAY 264

It's morning. Soft gray light slips over the tall redbrick wall. It stretches across the exercise yard and reaches through the high, barred windows. In a cell on the ground floor, the light shifts dark shapes into a small stool, a scrawny table, and a bed made of wooden boards with no mattress or blanket. On that bed, a thin, huddled figure, Helmuth, a boy of seventeen, lies awake. Shivering. Trembling.

It's a Tuesday.

The executioner works on Tuesdays.

∞

Memories drift through Helmuth's mind like clouds. Clouds that obscure his intense fear of what is to come. Slowly they shift into shapes. Helmuth. Holding Mutti's hand.

It's 1928, and Helmuth and his mother stroll up Luisenweg, the Hammerbrook street in Hamburg, where they live in a small flat next door to Helmuth's grandparents.

Helmuth is three. He is wearing short black pants and brown ankle boots that lace up. His older half brother Hans is eight. Hans is wearing short pants and ankle boots, too. So is Gerhard, who is seven. They are walking ahead of Mutti. Helmuth worries that his brothers will get lost, or worse, that they will have fun without him. Helmuth tugs on Mutti's hand. He wants to escape, wants to catch up with his brothers, but Mutti tugs back.

"No," she says. "Stay close, hold my hand. I don't want to lose you." That makes Helmuth feel dark inside. It isn't fair that he has to hold Mutti's hand and his brothers do not.

A street. Helmuth sees this, too. A noisy, crowded street. It's a parade. Brown-shirted men wearing red-and-black armbands and tall, black, shiny boots are marching. One swaggering Brownshirt bends over Helmuth. "What a big boy you are," he says. "Do you want to be a soldier for the Fatherland?"

Helmuth likes to play with toy soldiers. He forgets he is angry at Mutti. He nods and tells the Brownshirt, "Yes!"

The Brownshirt laughs a big booming laugh. He pats Helmuth's head. "A smart boy!" he says to Mutti. "And brave! Already he wants to fight for the Fatherland. And his eyes! So alert! Look how they take in everything."

"Yes," says Mutti in a proud voice. "He's very smart. And very brave, too."

∞

A loud bell clangs. Bright prison lights snap on. Helmuth sits, stretches. It's cold. He rubs his arms beneath his drab gray prison smock. He steps across the bare floor to the corner. Raises his smock, urinates into the slop bucket. For a moment, the cell grows thick with the stink from the bucket, and then thins, becomes ordinary again.

He lifts his bed against the wall, hooks it into place. Sits on the stool. Waits.

∞

Another memory. 1932.

It's nighttime. Helmuth is seven.

He lies on his back, tucked into bed between Hans and Gerhard. Helmuth hears Mutti dressing for work, the smooth wooden glide of bureau drawers, *Open, shut. Open, shut.*

His grandparents live in the flat next door. Through the wall, Helmuth hears a sonata from Opa's gramophone, a somber cello, warm and penetrating. Brahms.

It is a comfort to have Opa and Oma so close. That's what Mutti says, though sometimes she presses her lips together as she says it. And a help, too, since Mutti works nights at the nursing home and needs someone to check on her boys.

Moonlight floods the bedroom, shimmers the walls, opalescent. It makes Helmuth think about God and heaven. "Heaven goes on forever, doesn't it?" he whispers to his brothers.

It's always Gerhard who answers these questions, never Hans. "For infinity," says Gerhard, who is nearly four years older than Helmuth and knows about heavenly things like planets and stars and suns and moons. Gerhard likes precise words and numbers. Hans, five years older and with little patience for deep discussions, is already asleep — or pretending to be.

"How can something never end?" says Helmuth. "How does it go on and on, for infinity?"

"It just does," says Gerhard. "That's the way God made the universe, without beginning or end, in all directions."

"In all directions," repeats Helmuth, awestruck. "It makes me dizzy just thinking about it." He stops, thinks about the feeling. It isn't dizzy, not exactly. "I'm floating," he says.

"Then stop," says Gerhard.

"I can't stop. I'm going to float away, right this minute. Hold on to me, Gerhard."

"Don't be ridiculous. You're not going to float away." *Ridiculous* is one of Gerhard's favorite words.

"I will, too."

"No, you won't. There's such a thing as gravity. God made that, too, you know."

"But I am floating," says Helmuth. He rolls toward Gerhard, clutches his arm.

Gerhard pulls away. "You're ridiculous." He gives Helmuth a heave, shoves him toward the center of the bed, says in a practical voice, "When you're old enough to think about infinity, it won't make you float. Now go to sleep."

"But I like floating," whispers Helmuth into the shimmering darkness, and he does. It makes him feel drawn to God, as if God is drawing him toward heaven. He doesn't say this to Gerhard, because he doesn't want the feeling to disappear. Besides, he knows that Gerhard has stopped listening. That's the way Gerhard is, so able to remain anchored in the world.

And so Helmuth keeps floating toward heaven until he falls fast asleep.

Another memory.

School is out, and Helmuth is sitting on the floor playing with lead soldiers. He is next door at his grandparents' flat, because Mutti is still asleep, tired from her night shift. He forms two lines, with blue-clad French soldiers dug in on one side and gray-clad Germans attacking mercilessly on the other, just as they had fought on the Western front during the Great War.

Gerhard comes in and squats next to Helmuth. "Your right flank is in trouble," he says, pointing. "You can't keep your soldiers in a straight line. You must circle the enemy."

Helmuth tenses his jaw. He wants to argue with Gerhard, such a know-it-all he is, but he also sees his brother is right. Gerhard is always right. And so Helmuth moves a handful of Germans to protect the right flank.

Gerhard nods in approval. "That's better. You can't think in straight lines, not if you want to win."

Gerhard plops down on the stiff, flat sofa and cracks open his Karl May adventure novel. Helmuth crouches over the battlefield. He signals a charge to encircle the French. He imitates the sounds of artillery, exploding grenades, storms of shrapnel. He imagines billows of smoke as the brave German infantry attack with all their might. Their faces are dust-covered, their uniforms tattered.

Opa returns from his midday walk with a newspaper he has bought from a stall in the market square. He stands over Helmuth. "Who's winning?"

"The Germans," says Helmuth.

"Are the grenade launchers on their way?"

Helmuth nods vigorously.

"Your strategy is working. The French are trapped!" says Opa. "As it should have been, my boy. We should never have lost that war."

Oma bustles from the kitchen, carrying a teapot. The sharp scent of peppermint hovers in the air.

Opa sits, flaps open the newspaper, mutters about the headlines. "More head-cracking," he says. "More fighting between Communists and the Social Democrats and the Nazis. Each party promises jobs and a stronger economy."

"Can it get any worse?" asks Oma.

"Only if that lunatic Hitler comes to power," says Opa. "That will mean only one thing. War. That warmonger wants to make his mark on history."

Oma sits next to Opa and says, "Hitler frightens me. Those crazy eyes of his! And the way he knows exactly how to bring a crowd to hysteria."

For a long while, Opa and Oma sit in silence, his hand cupped over hers. Helmuth knows they are afraid of Adolf

Hitler, the leader of the Nazi Party. But he doesn't understand why they fear a man who wants to fight for Germany and make it better.

Helmuth rocks back on his heels, looks at his toy soldiers. If he were a soldier, he would fight bravely for Germany, just as Hitler fought in the Great War. He knows he would. He wouldn't be afraid.

∞

Footsteps. A rustling sound at the heavy blue door. Helmuth takes a great gulp of air. His heart pounds in his ears. The small latched window slides open. Please, God, no, not the executioner.

He sees an eye, a nose, half a mouth, half a face. The morning guard. Helmuth breathes again. Part of a prisoner's punishment is not knowing his execution date.

For a second their eyes meet. The guard pushes a cup of lukewarm malt coffee and a hunk of dry bread through the window. The window snaps shut.

Helmuth rejoices with relief. Gives thanks for the meager breakfast, for living to eat another morning meal. He knows letters have been written on his behalf, asking for clemency. Perhaps today will bring good news.

He gnaws on the hard, stale bread. Thinks about the breakfasts Mutti made — rye toast slicked with red currant jam made with berries that Helmuth picked himself. For supper they ate whatever Mutti could afford to cook that day, usually turnips and potatoes and cabbage. Helmuth and his brothers never went to bed hungry, Mutti made sure of that. But there were plenty of nights he wished for something more to eat.

He remembers how all of Germany was very poor and how Adolf Hitler promised to make everything better. Work and bread, that's what Hitler promised. Helmuth remembers the day Hitler was appointed chancellor, how the flat smelled of fresh rye bread and sausage and fried onions. Mutti celebrated. Everyone did.

∞

It is January 30, 1933, and nearly noon. It's almost dismissal time, and Helmuth is sitting on a hard wooden chair in the school auditorium. He is waiting for a special radio broadcast, a broadcast so important that the whole school has been gathered to listen.

At first his classmates sit quietly. As the minutes tick toward dismissal, the boys fidget, swinging their legs, tapping the floor with their heavy brown shoes, whispering and snickering when their teachers aren't looking.

Helmuth is filled with a sense of anticipation. Something big is about to happen, he can feel it, has felt it for days. It has something to do with Adolf Hitler, he is sure.

At the front of the auditorium, a fifth-grade teacher turns on the large radio. It crackles, and a stormy arpeggio from the final movement of Beethoven's *Moonlight Sonata* bursts forth. Its ferocity underscores the day's unquiet.

The teacher twists the knob, tunes in the German Reich station, the RRG. The radio squawks and then a newscaster speaks in a whisper. *"Guten Tag."* Good day, he says as if he doesn't want to disturb anyone, as if he is about to apologize for interrupting the school day.

But he doesn't apologize. Instead, his booming voice fills the auditorium. "Reich president Paul von Hindenburg has just formed a new government! Adolf Hitler, leader of the National Socialist Party, has been sworn into office as the new chancellor of the Reich!"

Martial music swells from the speakers. Something inside Helmuth swells, too. It has happened! Hitler is chancellor!

This is big news.

The room buzzes. Several older boys — sixth graders — leap to their feet. They clap one another on the back, thrust out their right arms in the Nazi salute, and bark, *"Heil* Hitler."

Helmuth is amazed at their boldness, even more amazed that not one teacher grabs them by the collar and shakes them, tells them to sit, to mind their manners.

Those swaggering boys belong to the Jungvolk, the Hitler Youth group for boys ten to fourteen. They sport brown shirts and swastika armbands, shiny belts and buckles, and best of all, daggers inscribed with the words *Blood and Honor* that glint from leather sheaths. The boys' eyes glitter.

"Did you hear that, Seligmann?" says one boy, leering.

There aren't many Jews in the school, but the Hitler Youth want the school yard *Judenfrei*. Jew-free. Benno Seligmann ignores their taunts. He gazes stonily ahead. But two angry red splotches glow on his cheeks.

The teachers ignore the Hitler Youth. They are too busy whispering sharply with the other teachers, fighting over the reasons why Germany is so desperate for Adolf Hitler. It's the same grown-up argument Helmuth has heard everywhere — between his mother and his grandparents; among his neighbors in the tenement; floating out of the teachers' room at school; and even among the older boys in the school yard.

"At last! Wait and see!" says one teacher. "Hitler will get Germany out of this mess! No more unemployment! No more inflation! He will bring jobs! Food for our tables!"

Another teacher shakes his head. "Bah! Hitler is a lunatic! He will bring war!"

And so the argument goes, back and forth, among the teachers. "Nonsense! Hitler wants peace! A strong Germany. Wait and see. He will restore our greatness!"

"The problem is that treaty. It's a sacrilege!"

Helmuth knows about the Treaty of Versailles, the peace agreement that ended the Great War in 1918. The treaty forced Germany to take all the blame for starting the war and to pay high reparations that made Germany poor. The treaty caused unemployment. Poverty. Inflation. And mostly it brought shame and humiliation to Germany.

A few teachers seem unconcerned by these arguments. They shrug their shoulders and stand idly with their hands in their pockets.

"What do I care? Hitler? What does it matter! All their promises sound the same! Nothing but lies!"

"Mark my words, Hitler won't last long. The German people won't be ruled by an idiot."

"Hitler will be hard on the Jews. I would not want to be a Jew in Germany."

"Hitler's just huffing and puffing about the Jews. He knows how to play up patriotism by giving people a common enemy."

"He makes people afraid, that's what he does. It's bad, the things that can happen when people become afraid."

Helmuth glances back at Benno Seligmann. Helmuth doesn't know many Jews, besides Benno and Benno's father, who owns a butcher shop. And there's Herr Kaltenbach, the baker, who gives Helmuth extra apple-cake trimmings.

Helmuth doesn't know why being a Jew is a big deal. Jews are children of Israel, God's first chosen people. That's what the Bible says. And that's what Helmuth's church teaches. He's a Mormon and belongs to the Church of Jesus Christ of Latter-day Saints. Mormons believe that people have a right to worship how, or where, or what they want. It's written right in the Thirteen Articles of Faith. Article Eleven, to be exact.

School is dismissed, and Helmuth runs outside. He looks for Gerhard and Hans, but he doesn't see them. The wind is biting cold and blowing from the north. It sweeps across the wide Elbe River and across Hamburg's channels and lakes.

Helmuth pulls his black woolen cap over his ears. The Hammerbrook streets teem with excitement. Storm troopers, wearing swastika armbands and tall, shiny jackboots, shout, *"Deutsches Volk erwache! Dem Nationalsozialismus gehört die Zukunft!"* German people awaken! The National Socialists are the future!

On the corner, several storm troopers, or the SA, as members of Hitler's private army are called, are passing out white leaflets that announce a victory parade through downtown Hamburg that night. "Do you know who Hitler is?" a storm trooper asks Helmuth.

"The leader of the National Socialist Party," says Helmuth. "And now he's our chancellor!"

"Smart boy!" says the storm trooper. He hands Helmuth a leaflet. "Come to the parade. Watch Germany awaken. Germany needs soldiers like you, to fight for the Fatherland."

Soldiers like you. The praise squares Helmuth's shoulders and he beams at the storm trooper. He snatches a leaflet, folds it, and slides it into his pocket.

All around it is snowing leaflets. The wind flutters them over the cobblestones like snow. The streets and sidewalks lie littered with white paper. The air is charged with excitement.

Helmuth feels electric with excitement, too. Someday he will fight for the Fatherland. He can feel it, knows in his heart that it's true.

The hallway outside his flat smells sweet, like sausage and fried onions. Helmuth drops his leather satchel near the door. In the kitchen Mutti stands at the stove and tends a large black skillet. She has dark circles under her eyes from not enough sleep. Mutti never sleeps enough. She is always tired — tired from working nights at the nursing home, tired from the elderly people and their demands, tired from scrubbing the nursing home floors, changing the patients' beds, from raising three boys alone.

Boys need a father, that's what Oma says. About that, Mutti never argues with her mother. She just says she's doing her best. But Helmuth knows Mutti is tired of Oma's advice, too. Mutti divorced Hans and Gerhard's father long ago, and she never married Helmuth's father. She doesn't like talking about that man, not one bit.

Helmuth clutches the leaflet as he watches Mutti brown the sausage and onions.

"Have you heard?" he asks. "About Hitler?"

Mutti smiles and taps the wooden spoon against the frying pan rim, then rests it on the counter. Helmuth senses that he is her favorite, though she would never say so. He senses that Gerhard and Hans know it, too.

"How can I not hear," says Mutti, "with all the shout-ing and marching? Who can sleep with all the excitement?

We're celebrating! With sausage and onions and sauerkraut. No more soup! Before you know it, we'll eat veal and potato dumplings and plum *Kuchen* every day!"

Plum cake! It's Helmuth's favorite. He takes his mother's good mood as a sign. He shores up his courage and shows her the leaflet. "*Bitte*, Mutti. Please, may I go?"

Mutti barely glances at the leaflet, doesn't even think it over. "*Ach, nay*," she says firmly. "You're too young."

"What if Hans and Gerhard take me?"

His mother hesitates. Helmuth uses her hesitation to dig in a toehold. "I'll stay by them. They will watch me. I'll be careful. We will be careful together."

Helmuth feels her giving in, but Mutti shakes her head, her dark brown hair billowing around her pretty face, her pale, tired face, and says, "*Nein*, it is *verboten*. I forbid you to go. You're not old enough. If something happened to you, I'd never forgive myself."

Helmuth crumples the leaflet, shoves it into his pocket. Darkness spreads through him. It isn't fair. "You let Hans and Gerhard go."

"Never mind about your brothers. They're older."

Helmuth scuffs at the floor with the toe of his shoe. His classmates will talk about the parade tomorrow. They will boast how their fathers took them. If only Helmuth had a father, things would be different. A father would let him go. A father would take Helmuth himself.

After supper, Mutti hums as she dresses for her job at the nursing home. Helmuth turns on Mutti's old radio. It's a small luxury to have a radio. Each month Mutti pays a tax to the Reichspost. That makes Oma click her tongue in disapproval, but the radio makes Mutti happy. Helmuth twists the dial and finds the Reich station, the RRG. He turns up the volume to tune out Mutti.

Over the radio, the RRG blares reports that the parade to celebrate Hitler's victory is under way. Thousands of flag-waving revelers are lining Germany's streets.

Helmuth glances at the clock. It's nearly seven. Hans and Gerhard are still not home. Helmuth can barely stand it. He feels certain that Mutti has allowed them to ride the train into the city center. He's convinced that they are jostling and pushing for a place on the sidewalk outside City Hall. And later, when they return home, they will rub it in, rub it in that they are old enough to participate in the celebration, and he is not.

Mutti kisses the top of Helmuth's head. "Your brothers will be home soon. Oma will come over to tuck you in," she says as she slips into her old, brown woolen coat.

It's so worn the edges are frayed, and so huge it swallows her up, so tiny is she.

At the door she trills her fingers good-bye. She feels bad, Helmuth can tell. Good. She *should* feel bad. He doesn't wave back, sits sullenly at the table. He's eight. Old enough to put himself to bed.

Helmuth turns up the volume on the radio, and the sounds of the parade fill the flat. He rests his chin on his hand and closes his eyes. He imagines the sidewalks jammed with revelers sporting swastika armbands and waving red, white, and black flags.

He hears the brass bands, too, and the living room gleams bright with the showy flutes and trumpets and trombones. He imagines the streets booming with Nazi storm troopers, hundreds of them, like distant thunder, marching straight-legged, twelve abreast, singing in echoing voices:

We have broken the bonds of servitude,
For us it was a great victory.
We shall march on and on,
Even if all is destroyed;
For today Germany shall hear us
And tomorrow the entire world.

Beneath the singing, Helmuth feels the drums. They stir his blood, call him to duty, make his legs long to leap away from the table, away from the radio, and run down to the inner city to join the marchers.

The flat door cracks open. It's Oma, wearing her housecoat and slippers, come to shoo Helmuth to bed. "Your mother spoils you, letting you stay up this late," Oma says, clucking her disapproval, but she leaves the radio on.

Helmuth crawls between the bedcovers. Shivers. It's cold without Gerhard and Hans to warm the bed. He thinks about the storm trooper earlier that day, how he said Germany needs soldiers. Soldiers like him, and he feels a deep love for all things German.

Helmuth tries to stay awake, but somehow he falls asleep. By morning the radio is quiet, and there lie Gerhard and Hans, fast asleep, anchored on either side of him.

Two nights later, Helmuth lies belly down on the livingroom floor, listening to Hitler's first speech over the radio. Hitler speaks plainly, in words easy to understand. Helmuth likes the sound of Hitler's voice, the way his rasping, barking voice pulses with energy.

It charges Helmuth up, makes his own heart beat with

fear as Hitler warns that Communism could destroy the Fatherland.

"It seeks to poison and disrupt in order to hurl us into an epoch of chaos," shouts Hitler. "Beginning with the family, Communists have undermined the very foundations of morality and faith, and scoff at culture and business, nation and Fatherland, justice and honor."

As their new chancellor, Hitler promises to protect Germany from Communists. He also promises to restore greatness to Germany, and he calls upon the German people to join in.

"Every class and every individual must help us create the new Reich," Hitler implores. "The National Government will preserve and defend those basic principles on which our country has been built. It regards Christianity as the foundation of our national morality and the family as the basis of national life."

Nation. Christianity. Morality. Family. Helmuth knows these things are very important.

The speech isn't very long, and at its end, Hitler prays, "May God Almighty give our work His blessing, strengthen our purpose, and endow us with wisdom and the trust of our people, for we are fighting not for ourselves but for Germany!"

"See?" says Mutti to Opa. "Hitler wants what's best for us."

Opa disagrees. "He wins the kingdom by flattery, just as the Bible warns us," he says, clicking off the radio. "But like it or not, Hitler's our chancellor now."

∞

And so the morning of day number 264 begins like every other morning on death row. Helmuth uses the slop bucket again, a handful of cut-up newspaper squares in his hand. He picks out the ones with Hitler's name and uses those to scrape himself.

∞

It's the end of February. Helmuth stirs awake as Mutti pulls up the bedcovers, smoothes them, bends over him, kisses his forehead.

"Mutti," he murmurs. "I was dreaming. About a sparrow." He doesn't want to open his eyes, doesn't want the dreamy, flying feeling to go away.

The bed sinks as Mutti sits beside him. "God watches over sparrows," she says softly. "The sparrow guides the soul to heaven." Her voice cracks a little, the way it does when she's anxious or troubled. "Now go to sleep," she says.

Mutti stands. She closes the bedroom door behind her, but Helmuth is wide awake now. He slips from bed, finds

Mutti sitting in the dark, listening to the radio, her hand over her mouth. The radio dial glows amber.

"Mutti, what's happened? Is it bad?"

She hushes him, pulls him onto her lap.

"The Reichstag is on fire!" blares the radio newscaster. "Burning out of control!"

This is shocking news. The Reichstag is the parliament building, the seat of government in Berlin. And now it's on fire.

"Adolf Hitler has pronounced the raging fire a Communist plot," cries the newscaster. "A plot to take over the German government! Germans must remain on ready alert!"

Helmuth's eyes open wide. "Are we in danger?"

"No, not us," says Mutti, pulling Helmuth close. "We're safe. They've already arrested the culprit."

"How do we know it's the right person?" asks Helmuth.

"They said so on the radio," says Mutti. "Hitler will protect us from Communists." She grasps his shoulders, steers him toward his bedroom. "Now go to bed."

Helmuth crawls between Gerhard and Hans, who are both sound asleep. The windows are closed against the cold, but Helmuth can hear the steady wail of a police siren. The police must be off to arrest Communists,

Helmuth assures himself. That's good. Jail is a good place for people who want to destroy the government.

More swastika flags hatch overnight, and the next day they flutter like bright birds from balconies and windows everywhere.

That afternoon Helmuth is eating bread with straw-berry jam when Opa's good friend Heinrich Worbs knocks loudly on the door. Brother Worbs is a peculiar old man, full of opinions, and everything he thinks he says in a loud voice. Brother Worbs just can't help himself, that's what Oma says. Helmuth likes the old man, shouts and all. Everyone does.

Brother Worbs waves a newspaper at Opa. The head-line blares in thick bold letters:

REICHSTAG BURNS!
COMMUNIST THREAT TURNED BACK!
HITLER DECLARES EMERGENCY DECREE
FOR PROTECTION OF STATE AND PEOPLE

"That carpet chewer!" cries Brother Worbs. "This new decree takes away our freedoms. Freedom of speech, gone! Freedom of the press, gone! Right to privacy, gone! The police can search our home, listen to our telephone calls, read our mail. And Hitler calls it protection! Sometimes I think the biggest winner is the biggest liar!"

Helmuth is shocked at Brother Worbs. Brother Worbs is a Mormon, just like Helmuth's family. Mormons are taught to respect their country and its leaders, even if one disagrees with them. "But the Communists burned our Reichstag," says Helmuth. "Hitler wants to protect us."

"It's not the Communists we must fear," says Brother Worbs. "Now we must fear what we say to our neighbors, what we say in our own homes, what we say over the telephone, what we write."

Opa tries to calm down Brother Worbs. "The decree is just a temporary inconvenience. A few freedoms aren't too much to sacrifice for safety."

Helmuth is surprised. It's the first time that he has heard his grandfather agree with Hitler.

"How can you say that?" says Brother Worbs. "Decree or no decree, I have always spoken the truth and I intend to continue to do so." He stands, thrusts his black felt hat onto his head.

Oma comes from the kitchen, wipes her hands on her apron. She motions to a chair at the table. "Come, Brother Worbs, sit."

But Brother Worbs won't stay, even though Oma asks two times. "I can't sit," he says. "I need to walk to settle my stomach."

Opa folds the newspaper and sets it down. He follows Brother Worbs to the door. "The decree won't last forever," says Opa.

"Nor will Hitler," says Brother Worbs. "That's what I pray for. I will never vote for a Nazi — no matter what they promise us."

Helmuth glances at the folded newspaper. He sees a photograph of the arsonist, a squinting, tousle-headed young man.

Oma peers over Helmuth's shoulder and clicks her tongue. "So young," she says. "I can't help but wonder how Hitler knew so quickly it was a Communist plot."

Helmuth can't stop staring at the culprit's face. "What will happen to him?" he asks Oma.

"The Nazis will find him guilty, no doubt," she says with a sigh. "They'll sentence him to death. That's what happens to traitors." She clicks her tongue again. "So young."

A week later, it's election day and Opa and Oma dress in their Sunday best. They stroll, arm in arm, to vote at the town hall.

Later they hear the results. The Nazi Party has gained a slight majority of seats in the Reichstag. Even people who despise Hitler have voted for Nazis, believing that the Nazis are the best protection from Communists.

Suddenly brown uniforms sprout up everywhere. Helmuth's teacher, Herr Zeiger, wears his SA uniform to school, and his Nazi Party badge winks in the light as he struts around the classroom. He holds up the *Völkischer Beobachter* — the Nazi Party newspaper — to Helmuth's class. The headline shouts in thick letters: *GERMANY, DEFEND YOURSELVES! DON'T SHOP AT JEWISH STORES!*

"Look what the Jews force us to do," says Herr Zeiger. "We must boycott the Jews in order to save the Fatherland."

Benno Seligmann's eyes narrow to pinpricks. It's no secret that the Jews hate Hitler and have called for an economic boycott. Jews all over the world have called on fellow Jews to boycott German goods in order to protest Hitler and the Jew-hating Nazi regime.

A classmate raises his hand. "My father says the Jews want to cripple the Fatherland's economy. Then they will take over."

"Exactly," says Herr Zeiger. "We have six million unemployed and three million more so poor that they can't put food on the table. Haven't we Germans suffered enough already? Do you want your mothers and fathers to suffer more?"

The students murmur in agreement. Helmuth thinks about Mutti, how hard she works, how tired she is. He doesn't want Mutti to suffer more. But all the things Herr Zeiger says about the Jews feel terribly wrong. Unease crawls over Helmuth.

Herr Zeiger glares at Benno and lowers his pointer, aiming it like a sword. "You see, class, Jews are traitors who want to destroy Germany. And what does the Jew Seligmann say to that?"

This shocks Helmuth. Benno Seligmann and his family, traitors? How can that be? Benno's father flies the gold-and-black flag of the Weimar Republic. A portrait of Reich president Hindenburg hangs in his butcher shop. Herr Seligmann fought in the Great War, where he was wounded and earned the Iron Cross for his bravery. He wears his lieutenant's uniform on national holidays.

Herr Zeiger doesn't wait for Benno to answer. He stalks around the room. "We must defend ourselves against bankruptcy! We must defend ourselves against Jews and their worldwide plot to take over Germany. We must fight back. If Jews want to boycott everything German, then we must boycott everything Jewish." He stops at Benno's desk and leans into his face. "After all, it's an eye for an eye, isn't it?"

"An eye for an eye makes the whole world blind, Herr Zeiger," says Benno.

This infuriates Herr Zeiger. His neck stretches into tight cords as he screams, "See how the Jew twists my words? See why Jews can't be trusted?"

Herr Zeiger grabs Benno's collar, drags him to a front-row seat. Shoves him into the chair. "Sit here," he says, his face purple with rage. "So we can keep an eye on you."

Benno sits, chin jutted. Doesn't look the least bit sorry. The next day Herr Seligmann and his wife come to school to meet with the head teacher. Benno retrieves his books and never comes to class again. He has transferred to the "Jewish school."

April in Hamburg is usually cool and damp, but the first day in April, a Saturday, is sunny. Mutti hands Helmuth a five Pfennig coin and tells him to buy a bag of apple-cake trimmings from Herr Kaltenbach.

Helmuth rushes outside and turns east onto Süderstrasse, the street where the Kaltenbach bakery and several other Jewish shops are housed. He stops short at the sight of brown-and-black uniforms. SS and SA men are everywhere. Plastering posters on walls. Stretching banners. GERMANS! DO NOT BUY FROM JEWS! WORLD JEWRY IS OUT TO DESTROY US!

There are Hitler Youth, too. Boys Helmuth knows, older boys from his school. Scrawling the word *JEW* in thick yellow paint and painting crude yellow outlines of the Star of David. On windows. Doors. Kaltenbach's bakery. Abraham Tobacco and Cigarette Import. Baumgarten Hats for Women. Cibulski Shoes. Galewski Women's and Children's Clothing. Seligmann's Butcher Shop.

Outside Herr Kaltenbach's bakery, a storm trooper stands. His legs are wide, his arms folded across his chest, his face tightly muscled. On the store window, the words *Germans! Don't buy from Jews!* have been painted. Over the front door, a yellow star glares thick with wet paint.

Helmuth spots Herr Kaltenbach inside, a short, round, kind-looking man with wisps of white hair and a spotless white apron. His wooden cases gleam, their paper-lined trays heaped with pastries and breads and cakes.

Herr Kaltenbach paces back and forth, rubbing his hands together. He reaches into his apron pocket, extracts a white handkerchief, and mops his glistening forehead.

Helmuth clutches the coin and starts for the door.

"Juden Laden," growls the storm trooper. "This is a Jewish shop."

Just then, there are shouts. Helmuth glances across the street. Benno Seligmann's father is standing outside his shop, wearing, of all things, his lieutenant's uniform from the Great War, medals and all. He has a bucket and is washing the slurs from his window, smearing the yellow paint into huge wet circles.

"*Halt!*" barks a storm trooper.

Herr Seligmann turns and says calmly, "My windows are dirty. Surely I have a right to wash my store windows."

The street grows quiet. The air ripens, smells rotten.

Helmuth wants to beg Herr Seligmann to stop. But Herr Seligmann dunks the scrubcloth into the bucket, wrings it out, and continues wiping the window. Four snarling storm troopers rush in. They topple Herr Seligmann, batter him, pile blows on him, kick him. He curls into a ball, protecting his head and stomach.

Helmuth cries out at the thuds of fists, the hard grind of boots against bone, the grunts, the groans, and then silence.

The Nazis drag their arms across their damp foreheads, looking strangely flushed, exhilarated. They suck on their knuckles and brush the dirt from their uniforms. Herr Seligmann's rumpled body lies motionless on the sidewalk.

A sick feeling rises in Helmuth's stomach. His mouth tastes sour. He glances at the bakery. The window shades are drawn, the store dark, Herr Kaltenbach gone. Helmuth heads down the street. He buys the cake trimmings from a German baker who looks most pleased at all his new customers.

Helmuth hands Mutti the package, and when she peers inside, she notices the trimmings right away. "These are not Herr Kaltenbach's," she says.

Helmuth swallows hard. He tells Mutti about the storm troopers, the boycott, the banners, the painted Stars of David, and Herr Seligmann. The words feel dirty, as dirty as a lie in his mouth.

"How dare that brown-shirted pest tell us where to shop!" says Oma. "I will shop where I please!"

"I don't want you to take any chances," says Opa sternly. "Do you hear me? I forbid it. This hatred can't last forever."

"And until then?" says Oma.

Opa reaches for a cake trimming, takes a bite. "These aren't so bad." He offers one to Helmuth, but Helmuth shakes his head no. He fears he will throw up if he eats one bite.

May. A Saturday afternoon. Opa gives Helmuth and Gerhard and Hans money for the movies. They buy their tickets and climb into the balcony seats. They wait for the feature, a western, to begin.

Helmuth loves westerns. He loves the American Wild West, its cowboys, the gunfights, the fistfights. He loves the feeling of losing himself in the action, the same way he feels when he reads his brother's Karl May adventure novels, which are also set in America.

The theater lights dim. A black-and-white newsreel flickers on the screen. The boys and girls stir, restless for the main feature. But the newsreel interests Helmuth. This one shows a huge bonfire that took place in the courtyard outside the university library in Berlin. Students wearing uniforms and swastika armbands are tossing books onto the burning pyre. The books arc, and their covers spread like a bird's wings as they soar toward the fire.

"From now on," intones the narrator, "Germans will read only German books by German authors, books that promote strong, traditional German ideals. We will not have our minds poisoned by Jews and others who promote liberal ideas."

In the newsreel the students cheer. All around Helmuth, boys and girls cheer, too, rocking the balcony with their stamping of feet.

Helmuth feels sickened. He thinks about the Karl May adventure stories. What if the Nazis ban the Karl May westerns, what if they call them un-German because they are set in the American Wild West?

His stomach in turmoil, Helmuth doesn't enjoy the movie. He just can't lose himself in the story. Later, at the flat, he hurries to his bedroom and closes the door. He sits on his bed and stares at the bookshelf. He reaches for his brother's novels, pulls them from the shelf. He doesn't want to hide the books, but he fears he must.

Helmuth stashes them beneath the bed. He finds Gerhard in the living room and sits beside him on the couch. He feels guilty about the hidden books. He knows he's supposed to honor his country and his leaders, and that means to obey, honor, and sustain its laws. That's what the Mormons' Twelfth Article of Faith tells him. But must he obey a law that feels wrong?

"Gerhard," says Helmuth slowly. "Is it ever all right to do something you're not supposed to?"

"What kind of thing are you talking about? Do you mean something illegal? Breaking the law?"

Helmuth thinks about that. "Yes," he says. "Is it ever all right to break the law?"

"Breaking the law is serious. But God gave us free agency," says Gerhard. "That means we have the right to choose our own actions. If you choose to break the law to help someone else or keep someone from harm, then it's justified."

Helmuth feels hopeful for a second, because Gerhard is right. God did give him free agency. Helmuth tries to reason why reading a forbidden book might help someone else. He can't. "Suppose it's not to help anyone?"

"If it's for your own convenience and other people could be harmed, then it's wrong."

Helmuth weighs this answer, tries hard to determine if reading a banned book could harm another person. He doesn't think so. "What if it's for your own convenience but no one will be harmed?"

Gerhard's voice turns harsh, judgmental. "Then it's selfish and wrong. You should know better." He looks at Helmuth sternly. "Are you thinking of breaking the law? You'd better tell me."

"I've hidden your Karl May books," Helmuth admits, exasperated. "They're set in America, and that makes them un-German. I don't want to burn them, and I don't want you to get in trouble."

Gerhard laughs. "You don't have to hide them," he says. "Karl May is Hitler's favorite author, you know. Hitler likes the Wild West, too."

Helmuth didn't know. He feels much better. But still, he finds Gerhard annoying, the way he knows it all, the way he is so sure of himself, the way he can tell right from wrong as surely as if he were solving long division.

∞

The morning sun moves higher on the wall. From down the corridor, Helmuth hears footsteps. White-hot fear blazes down his back. The footsteps pass his cell, stop several doors away. The fear turns to cold sweat. It's not him.

The rattle of keys.

A door swinging open. A guard's voice. "Come with us. It is time." That's what the guards say when they escort a prisoner to the low redbrick execution chamber in the courtyard, where the guillotine waits.

A wailing sets up. "No!"

Helmuth's stomach turns. He hears blows, the dull thuds of a truncheon, the kick of boots, the shackling of handcuffs.

A door slams.

Sobs. Footsteps. The drag of feet.

A minute passes. Two minutes. Three.

Then, in the distance, metal against metal. The guillotine snaps its iron jaws with a clang that rings throughout the prison.

Silence.

Helmuth's insides turn to water. He rushes to the slop bucket, throws up. He drags his arm across his mouth. He kneels beneath the cell window, closes his eyes, and prays for the soul of his neighbor.

Helmuth believes in prayer, believes in God, has always believed in God, even now doesn't believe that God has abandoned him but has grown closer. For not one sparrow is forgotten before God. That's what the Bible says.

And so Helmuth does not give up hope as he prays, "O my heavenly Father, if it be possible, open the minds and hearts of these people: nevertheless, not as I will, but as Thou wilt."

He feels something. His chest swells. A warm calmness fills him. God is listening, of this Helmuth is sure. He squeezes his eyes tighter, repeats the last words, chants them fervently, asThouwiltasThouwiltasThouwilt, until they wrap around him and the floating feeling comes.

∞

It's April 1935, and spring has come to Hamburg. Helmuth hears it in the crackling gray ice floes that drift through the rivers and narrow canals. He sees it in the mallard ducks that bob, bottoms up, in the Alster lake and in the return of the robin.

Helmuth sees spring in Mutti's eyes, too. She has a new boyfriend, the tall, dark-haired, mustachioed Hugo Hübener. Mutti stays out late dancing with Hugo, and some mornings when Helmuth awakens, Mutti is humming in the kitchen and Hugo is sitting at their table. He wears his brown-and-black SS uniform with its blue collar insignia that says he's a Rottenführer, a noncommissioned corporal.

Before long the Rottenführer is sitting at their table every morning, taking up all the air in the flat. He stretches out, clasps his hands behind his head, elbows wide, and crosses his gleaming black jackboots at the ankles, saying, "The Führer this, and the Führer that."

Without asking, Hugo turns in Mutti's old radio for a new People's Receiver, the Volksempfünger VE 301. It is a cheap brown plastic radio, with a simple dial and no shortwave so that it only receives German stations. "See?" says Hugo proudly. "The 301 stands for January 30, the day Hitler became our leader. Thanks to the Führer, every German can afford a new radio. All of Germany can tune in the Führer."

It grinds Helmuth's stomach, the way Hugo makes all the decisions, as if he is the father. He decides what Mutti will make for breakfast and dinner and asks Helmuth if his homework is done. And now Hugo has even decided on the radio. Helmuth cannot understand what Mutti sees in a man like Hugo, but Hugo seems here to stay.

And stay he does. By 1937, Hugo has moved in with them, and one morning, he announces in his booming voice that the flat is too small. There's not enough *Lebensraum* — Hitler's favorite word — for living space. "All Germans need *Lebensraum*," Hugo says. "I have found us a new flat, Emma. We're moving."

And just like that, Mutti packs up everything — the dishes, the pots and pans, the uneven chairs, the brown wooden table, the worn armchair, the scratched-up black oak table lamp, the two wooden bedsteads. They move to a first-floor apartment at Sachsenstrasse 42.

Helmuth misses the comfort of his grandparents next door, their quiet flat where he doesn't feel as though he's holding his breath, where he can escape to do his homework in peace. It's different for Hans and Gerhard. They're old enough to bicycle with their friends to Cuxhaven on the North Sea where they camp overnight and dive for mussels that they cook on the beach.

But Mutti is happy, happier than Helmuth ever remembers. She sings as she puts away the dishes, stacks the pots and pans beneath the sink, polishes the furniture. Her eyes glow as she tells Helmuth that everything will work out just fine, that Hugo wants to be a father to him.

"Wait and see," she says. "We will marry, and when we do, Hugo will adopt you. You will be his son."

The thought turns Helmuth cold inside. "I'm twelve, going on thirteen," he says. "I don't need a father anymore."

"Every boy needs a father," says Mutti.

"Gerhard and Hans do just fine without one," says Helmuth. "And so do I."

"Just promise me you'll give Hugo a chance," says Mutti. "He wants what's best for you."

A sensation of unease rises in Helmuth's stomach, swims about. He doesn't like Hugo. He resents his presence in their flat, but he can't tell Mutti no, and so he says yes, for Mutti's sake.

In 1938, Helmuth graduates from primary school and starts at the Oberbau, the middle school at Brackdamm. On his first day, Helmuth carries his satchel into the classroom and sets it on a desk near the window. The schoolroom is plain, but the wall paint is fresh and the wooden floorboards newly oiled and the desks worn. The room feels well-lived-in.

A bright swastika flag hangs above the teacher's chair. Brand-new textbooks sit, stacked on the desk. The other boys file in, most wearing Hitler Youth uniforms. The classroom grows noisy, and Helmuth feels lost in the din. He doesn't know anyone, so he prefers to stay off to himself, to take it all in.

Suddenly the classroom door slams shut, and the room falls silent. A short, trim man with fashionably slicked brown hair walks crisply to the front. He has wide shoulders and muscular arms. He turns on his heel and faces the class at attention, like a soldier.

The boys leap to their feet. They shoot their hands forward and cry out, "*Heil* Hitler!" It never feels right to say "*Heil* Hitler" instead of "Good morning," but it's the rule, and so Helmuth follows.

The man raises his dark eyes to look at Adolf Hitler's portrait, as if invoking the Führer's blessing over his class. He then lifts his arm nonchalantly, a bored wave it seems, and returns the Hitler salute.

"Be seated," he says and then he introduces himself as their new teacher, Herr Vinke. "An exciting year awaits you," he says. "Never has there been a more exciting time to be young and to be a student. Thanks to the Führer, you will learn the new thinking in Germany."

He thumps the textbooks with his knuckles. "The National Socialist educational program surpasses anything of its kind in history. You see, my boys, the reality is this: It is your job to shape the fate of our Fatherland."

Herr Vinke picks up a stack of books and passes them out. "We will begin our study with the unlikeness of men," he says.

This makes Helmuth squirm inside, the same way he squirms when Hugo laughs over cartoons that depict Jews in an ugly manner.

But the lesson isn't about race. It's about the different mental and spiritual traits of men, traits such as courage and honor and duty. These are questions that Helmuth has often pondered at night when he lies in bed.

Helmuth grows more interested and listens intently. "For some, courage and loyalty are nothing but great stupidities," says Herr Vinke. "They would rather be live cowards than dead heroes."

Helmuth reflects on those words. He knows he's loyal, but he wonders if he is also brave, if he has what it takes to be a hero.

Herr Vinke continues, "Others, however, cannot live without honor and prefer death to cowardice. They want their death to stand for something."

He picks up a large, scrolled print. He unrolls it and holds it out for the class to see. Helmuth is intrigued by the sinking ship, by the drowning sailor who clings to the naval flag, by the debris floating about. Even as the sea rages around him, the brave sailor keeps the flag safely above him and the water.

"This painting is called *Fulfilling His Last Duty*," says Herr Vinke. "It illustrates one's duty to raise high the flag, to never let it fall. This is what it means to be a good German. A good German is loyal. Honorable. Brave. Courageous. Willing to sacrifice himself for his country."

Helmuth knows these things. He knows that a good German puts loyalty and self-sacrifice ahead of all personal interests. But there is something about the drowning naval soldier that bothers Helmuth. He raises his hand to speak.

Herr Vinke calls on him, and Helmuth stands. "Wouldn't it be better, sir, to grab a piece of the floating wood even if it means letting go of the flag? This way, you might live to fight another day for your country."

This enrages Herr Vinke. He pinches his lips shut for a long moment, and when he finally speaks, his words are clipped and cutting. "Sit down! You have completely failed to understand a soldier's duty! The greatest honor for any soldier is to die for his country rather than to let the flag fall. For the flag represents the Fatherland — and if the flag falls, Germany falls! Is that what you want?"

"No, sir," says Helmuth. He feels embarrassed and confused.

"You are a troublemaker. I should mark this down in your Party record book, but I will not. Instead, you have earned the class an extra homework assignment."

Herr Vinke announces that the class must write a five-hundred-word essay with the title, "Adolf Hitler, Savior of the Fatherland."

Helmuth's classmates cast angry glances at Helmuth as they snap open their notebooks and copy down the title.

Helmuth tries to make sense of what just happened. He opens his notebook, dutifully copies down the assignment as anger swells inside him. Anger that Herr Vinke misunderstood his question, anger that Herr Vinke now thinks him a coward. Anger and humiliation beat inside Helmuth with a pulse all their own.

That night Helmuth sits at the kitchen table, feeling dark, chewing on his pencil. His paper is blank except for its title and opening sentence.

It wasn't fair, the way Herr Vinke twisted Helmuth's question, the way Herr Vinke made the whole class suffer. Now the entire class is angry at Helmuth — and who can blame them? Helmuth could kick himself for raising his hand, for asking that question.

Hugo Hübener comes up from behind. He rests his hand on Helmuth's shoulder, startling him. Hugo's hand feels gentle but strong. Hugo leans over Helmuth's shoulder and reads the first sentence out loud. "God has blessed our Fatherland by giving us Adolf Hitler."

He squeezes Helmuth's shoulder in approval. "A good start, my boy!"

Helmuth cringes. He hates it when Hugo calls him "my boy."

"His homework mocks God," says Gerhard matter-of-factly. He doesn't look up from his physics book. Now seventeen, Gerhard has begun classes at the Technicum where he studies electrical engineering. He's seldom home anymore, since he also works at the MützenFabrik, a factory that makes stiff military hats, the kind with the visor in front. The long hours and hot, smelly work make him tired and cross. Helmuth wishes his other brother were at home, too, to say what he thinks. But Hans is a shipbuilding apprentice at the dockyards, and Helmuth rarely sees him at all.

"God and country go together," says Hugo.

"They do," says Gerhard. "But that essay isn't about God and country. It makes an idol out of Hitler. And anyone who makes an idol out of a leader mocks God."

"It does *not* mock God!" says Hugo. "The Fatherland is a gift to us from God. And God has blessed the Fatherland by giving us a leader like Hitler, who has the strength and resolve to lead Germany out of this mess. You should honor your country, and that means honoring your leaders. Doesn't that church of yours teach you anything?"

Helmuth feels anger rise inside at Hugo's biting remark. Hugo isn't a Mormon. How dare he criticize their church! Hugo doesn't even go to church. Not even when Mutti pleads.

Gerhard's eyes brighten the way they always do when he stands up to Hugo. "I do honor my country, Hugo, the way my church tells me I should. Every day I honor my country by obeying, honoring, and sustaining its laws. I am a good German, no matter what I think of the Führer."

"Are you insulting the Führer?" demands Hugo.

"No," says Gerhard. "I am insulting that essay."

Helmuth can't take their arguing anymore. He can't afford a bad grade — or a bad mark — in his Party record book, because that would keep him from getting a good job later on.

And so before Hugo can respond, Helmuth smacks his hand against the table. "It's *my* homework!" he shouts. "And I'll write what I need to write!"

Hugo and Gerhard stop arguing. They are surprised at Helmuth's outburst.

"A savior is somebody who rescues someone or something from harm or danger," Helmuth begins. "That's what Hitler has done. He has rescued the Fatherland from poverty, unemployment, and inflation — just as he promised he would."

Hugo's eyes widen with pleasure, but Gerhard doesn't say a word. He stacks his books loudly and stalks to the door. He yanks the door handle hard, and then lets the door slam behind him.

The slamming door sounds like a pistol shot. Helmuth looks to Mutti, who is standing in the kitchen doorway. He wants her to say something, to defend Gerhard because that's what mothers do for their children, but she doesn't. Suddenly Helmuth can't remember the last time she spoke up for one of them. Hugo always has the final word. And now Helmuth feels just as cowardly. He didn't speak up for Gerhard, either.

Mutti's face crumples. She lowers herself onto the

couch, buries her face in her hands. "Why can't you two let each other be? Why must you fight?"

Hugo sits beside her, draws her to him, kisses the top of her head. "Men like to fight," he says. "That's the way we are. It's in our blood. But don't worry. Gerhard will come around. You'll see."

And then to Helmuth, Hugo beams. "But you, my boy, have the right attitude! A born leader, that's what you are! A man to watch! You will go far!"

Helmuth blocks out the sound of Hugo's praise. He doesn't feel like a leader, a man to watch. He squirms inside as he stares at the words, *God has blessed our Fatherland by giving us Adolf Hitler.* Is Gerhard right? Does it make an idol out of Hitler? Does it mock God?

Every day, it seems, the Nazis hang more portraits of Adolf Hitler. Town squares and buildings are renamed after him. They evoke his name in praise and even in prayers, giving thanks to the Führer for getting Germany back on its feet, for jobs, for the new factories that produce everything from tanks and airplanes and guns to the cheap People's Radio.

Helmuth knows he's supposed to support his country and its leaders, and yet the Nazis feel dark and threatening, too. Every day, it seems, the Nazis pass more laws against the Jews. Helmuth sees terrible signs that read:

JEWISH SWINE and JEWS OUT, JEWS DIE. In school, Helmuth must pass tests that show he understands the differences between inferior races such as the Jews and the superior Aryan race. How does such meanness and hate build a better Germany?

Helmuth sits at the table, tapping his pencil impatiently as he wrestles with his feelings. Finally he pushes them down and begins to write. He doesn't think about the meaning behind the words, just writes — writes what Herr Vinke wants to hear, writes what will earn a high mark.

The inside of Helmuth's head feels like crashing cymbals. The words, the sentences, waver, bang apart, come back together again until at last he's finished. He stares at the handwritten pages and feels worse than a coward. He feels like a traitor, a traitor to his brother but mostly a traitor to himself. A traitor to his true feelings.

That night Gerhard's side of the bed remains empty. Helmuth turns on his stomach, then flops back again, thinks about Gerhard, of how sure he is of everything, even what he wants to do with his life. As Helmuth drifts off to sleep, he wonders about his own future and what he has been put on this earth to do.

Several days later, Herr Vinke returns the graded essays. Helmuth has earned a high mark, with only a brief comment, *Well done.* He stuffs the essay into his satchel and heads home. The satchel feels heavy, but not from the weight of books. It is heavy from the weight of the graded paper, the weight of Vinke's praise.

In spring 1938, Austria is reunited with Germany, and near the end of the school year, a Nazi official, an SS officer, accompanies Herr Vinke to class. The official introduces himself as Asmus, the senior district director of the Hitler Youth in the Hammerbrook neighborhood.

"As you know, all eligible young people are required by law to join the Hitler Youth," Herr Asmus says crisply. "It's your duty to serve the Fatherland. Most of you already belong. I am here today to sign up stragglers."

Helmuth is the first to be called. He stands, wishes he could drop through the floor. There was a time when Helmuth longed to join, but living with Hugo has changed all that.

Herr Asmus looks down at his orderly notes. "Name?" he asks, though Helmuth can see his name printed there, plain as day, in the non-member column.

Helmuth stands straight, arms at his side, takes a deep breath, says, "Guddat, Helmuth Guddat."

The director asks general questions about Helmuth's family and their political beliefs, which Helmuth answers briskly:

"*Nein,* I am not a member of the Hitler Youth."

"*Nein,* my mother is not a Communist."

"*Ja,* my mother's name is Emma Guddat Kunkel."

"My mother is divorced from her first husband, Johannes Kunkel."

"I have two older half brothers, Hans and Gerhard Kunkel."

"My mother never married my father."

Herr Asmus looks up at Helmuth. A mocking smile crosses his face.

"She is engaged to marry Hugo Hübener," says Helmuth.

At this, Asmus arches one eyebrow, says, "Hübener, you say? The Rottenführer?"

"*Ja.*"

Asmus nods in approval. "*Ach, ja,*" he says. "The Rottenführer is a good Nazi." He pries no further. He scribbles a notation and then hands Helmuth a paper to sign and another to get signed at home.

Helmuth takes the first paper and signs his name, assuring that he is 100 percent Aryan, not one drop of Jewish blood. He has the documentation to prove it for six generations.

"Welcome," says Asmus. "Here's the address where your *Kameradschaft* meets." He slides a piece of paper toward Helmuth. "Report Wednesday at seven o'clock sharp."

Mutti doesn't fuss at all, and the next day Hugo surprises Helmuth with a brown Jungvolk shirt and the ten Pfennig for dues. "Few men are born to lead. The rest are born to follow," he tells Helmuth. "You are a leader, my boy. I can tell."

All that spring and into the summer, Helmuth busies himself with the Jungvolk — its meetings and games and weekend hiking and camping trips.

Oma and Opa complain when Helmuth misses church, and that's something that Helmuth misses, too.

But Hugo tells Oma and Opa that it's Helmuth's duty. "God expects young people to serve the Fatherland," he says. "It's one of the sacrifices young Germans must make for their country." He beams as he looks at Helmuth. "Isn't that right, my boy?"

∞

The sound of feet ring outside Helmuth's cell. A key turns in the lock, and the door swings open. Helmuth catches his breath, releases it slowly. It's the morning guard. Exercise time.

Helmuth picks up his slop bucket, carries it outside, waits his turn to empty it, hose it out. Everything feels magnified in the prison yard — the crisp autumn air, the grass, the trees, the leaves red yellow orange, the sky blue clouds white sun yellow so much color so much air so much light. So much everything it hurts.

The guard barks a command. The prisoners trudge clockwise around the prison yard, marching single file on the worn path, their gray prison smocks billowing like the wings of birds. It's verboten to speak to other prisoners.

Helmuth keeps his head down, avoids their faces, doesn't want to see the new faces, or the missing faces after the executioner has done his work. He looks down his thin legs his knobby knees his worn leather shoes no shoelaces the grass the dirt. Thinks instead about his two best friends, Rudi Wobbe and Karl-Heinz Schnibbe. Sees Rudi's worried face, Karl's big grin, a face comfortable with smiling.

The boys lived in different neighborhoods and attended different schools, but they belonged to the same Mormon church. There aren't many Mormons in Hamburg, and their church is housed in a factory building in the St. Georg district of Hamburg. It seemed as though the three boys were

destined to be friends, from the day they met in primary class
at church.

∞

By summer 1938, the city parks have sprouted signs forbidding Jews to enter. Churches, too, for the Nazis declare that even Jews who convert to Christianity are still Jews.

Such a sign is even posted at Helmuth's church to protect the church from Jews. This is what the branch president says after he sees the Gestapo sitting in the back of the church, taking notes. The Nazis watch everything — churches, schools, places people work. But church members protest and tear down the sign after one week.

The Hitler Youth's Jungvolk meetings keep Helmuth busy, and several weeks pass before Helmuth sees his friend Rudi Wobbe. When he does, it's by chance that they meet. Helmuth is sitting on a park bench, reading a detective novel.

Rudi sits himself down next to Helmuth. "Where have you been?" he asks.

Helmuth dog-ears the page and closes the book. "Jungvolk," he says.

Rudi scowls. "You joined?"

Helmuth nods, and Rudi grows silent, giving the bobbing mallards his undivided attention. Helmuth knows

Rudi had a bad experience in the Jungvolk, that he quit after his squad had roughed him up. Karl Schnibbe's experience wasn't much better, except that Karl was expelled after he beat up his zealous platoon leader. Karl has no patience for Nazis — or bullies.

"So you're a Nazi now?" says Rudi.

Helmuth stares at a pair of ducks, circling each other. Admires how smooth and unruffled they look, but beneath the water, they're paddling furiously.

"Hugo bought me the shirt and paid the dues," he says to Rudi. "I couldn't refuse. But don't mistake *me* for a Nazi. I'm nothing like Hugo."

He doesn't want to tell Rudi that there are things he actually likes about the Jungvolk: the weekend hiking and camping trips that take him away from the Sachsenstrasse flat that feels so full of Hugo. There's also a special Hitler Youth section for older boys that intrigues him — the HJ-Streifendienst, a patrol force whose members act as junior Gestapo. He likes the idea of detective work, of working to serve and protect the public. But that doesn't make him a Nazi.

If Helmuth were a detective, he'd arrest real criminals, not the ordinary men and women who criticize Hitler or the Nazi Party and find themselves denounced by friends and neighbors.

Helmuth glances back at Rudi, can tell he's brooding. "You'd like this book," Helmuth says, changing the subject. He reads the title out loud: *Lord Lister, genannt Raffles, der grosse Unbekannte.* "It's about a gentleman thief who helps honest men ruined by swindlers."

Silence.

"The thief twists the law," says Helmuth. "But he does so for honorable reasons, to bring dishonest men to justice. He robs the robbers!"

"Like Robin Hood?" says Rudi.

"Exactly!" says Helmuth. Helmuth has missed his friend, finds himself irritated that Jungvolk duty has kept them apart. Suddenly Helmuth is struck with an idea, one that will restore their friendship. "Rudi, we should start our own detective agency," he says.

Rudi looks at him incredulously. "And play detective like children?"

"No," says Helmuth. "Have you not noticed all the unsolved crimes in the newspaper? The police say they need our help, that it's our duty to report suspicious activity."

"Do you mean spy on our neighbors?" Rudi's eyes narrow with disgust. "The Nazis have enough informers."

"No! Real crimes. You know, robberies and murders."

"We can't do that. We're not old enough. The police will laugh at us."

"They won't laugh," says Helmuth. "Not when they see that we can think like adults." He taps his head with his forefinger. "And we have an advantage. We're young, so criminals won't suspect us. We'll get more information that way."

"It's impossible," says Rudi. "You're talking about the Gestapo." He shudders. "I'd rather steer clear of them. A lot of people disappear after the Gestapo visit."

"I'm not afraid of the Gestapo," says Helmuth. He straightens his shoulders and juts out his chin. "When we crack our first case, we'll be famous! Maybe they'll even offer us a reward. Or a job! Come on, it can't hurt to try."

Helmuth watches Rudi's face. Everything Rudi thinks shows on his face. Before Rudi says so, Helmuth can see his face shift into agreement. "Sure," says Rudi. "Okay. Why not? We'll be detectives."

The discomfort between the two friends has fallen away. Helmuth crooks his arm around Rudi's neck. "This will be fun."

The next day Helmuth hands Rudi a small card. The card reads, *LORD LISTER DETECTIVE AGENCY.*

Rudi holds the card by its edges and whistles under his breath. "You made these yourself? They look real!"

"They are real," says Helmuth.

Rudi reads further. "Helmuth Guddat, Agent Number 1. Rudi Wobbe, Agent Number 2." He grins, tucks his card into his wallet.

"Come on," says Helmuth. "Let's go down to the police station and see what crimes they have for us."

Helmuth and Rudi head north toward the local police station at Hammer Deich 57. An odd, watchful silence hangs over the foreboding brick building. They stand outside and watch as four SS men exit the front doors, green files tucked under their arms, striding toward Grevenweg. Two other men, wearing the coats and hats of Gestapo agents, stride past without even a glance at the boys.

Helmuth thought about wearing his Hitler Youth uniform, but settled upon wearing good brown trousers and a white shirt. The trousers and shirt make him look more grown-up. He walks crisply to the heavy wooden door and pulls it open.

"Maybe this isn't such a good idea," says Rudi, firmly rooted on the sidewalk. He is also dressed in his best dark trousers and a white shirt.

"Come on," urges Helmuth. "You don't have to say a word. I'll do the talking."

"What are you going to say?"

"I don't know. I'll figure it out inside."

Rudi traipses behind Helmuth. The foyer feels cool and dark as they walk down the hall, reading the gold-lettered names and titles on the doors. Helmuth stops outside a detective's office and reads the name: Inspector Becker. It seems as good as any other name.

Helmuth turns the doorknob. A blond secretary sits at a gleaming wooden desk. Helmuth introduces himself, asks to speak with Inspector Becker. She hesitates, but Helmuth tells her that he and Rudi wish to do their duty as citizens. She leaves her desk, raps on the door behind her, and disappears inside. When she returns, she ushers the boys into a wood-paneled office that smells of cigarette smoke.

A balding man with strands of dark hair combed carefully across his head sits behind another wooden desk polished to a sheen that reflects the glow of the lamp. With his white shirt and red bow tie, Inspector Becker looks more like a banker than an inspector. He sets a green folder flat on the desk blotter, motions to a pair of dark leather chairs. The boys sit, and Becker leans back. He thrums the tips of his fingers together, smiles thinly, and says, "So you boys are here to do your duty as citizens?"

Herr Becker has a broad, blunt face, and Helmuth

notes that his eyes don't match his smile. "Yes, sir," he says.

The smile fades. "Do you have information for me? Perhaps you know somebody who is breaking the law? A neighbor or relative or teacher, perhaps? Something you've overheard? Some suspicious activity?"

"No, sir, nothing like that. My partner and I" — Helmuth nods at Rudi — "want to help the police solve crimes."

Becker's expression changes, grows less pleasant. "I am a busy man, with no time to waste with childish games." He picks up a folder, taps it against the desk, sticks it on top of a short stack of files.

"This isn't a game, sir," says Helmuth. "We think like adults, even better than adults, and because we're —" He starts to say children, catches himself, starts over, says, "Because we're young, adults let their guard down. They're less cautious about what they say. That works to our advantage."

Becker's chair squeaks as he sits back, eyes Helmuth, then Rudi carefully. "I consider myself a good judge of people," he says at last. "You're smart. Curious. Not afraid to take initiative. I'll bet you can put two and two together."

Helmuth leans forward. "We can."

Inspector Becker tugs open a desk drawer, fingers through several files, takes out a slim folder, spreads it open on his desk. He thumbs through newspaper clippings, pulls one out. "Here's an open case. A streetwalker was murdered in Rothenburgsort."

Helmuth looks wide-eyed at Rudi, at the luck of it all, then back at the inspector. "We know that neighborhood." Helmuth thumbs at Rudi. "That's where my partner lives."

The inspector nods. "See what you can find out. Let me know." He pours himself a cup of coffee, offers one to Helmuth and Rudi.

Helmuth shakes his head and says, "No thanks." Mormons don't drink coffee, though Helmuth likes its deep, rich smell. Inwardly he feels pleased that Becker asked. It's a sign that the inspector takes him seriously.

Over the next several days, Helmuth and Rudi prowl the Rothenburgsort streets, engaging the local shopkeepers and customers in conversation about the night of the stabbing. Helmuth keeps careful notes. He jots down each detail, no matter how small or insignificant. Afterward, he and Rudi put the details together, shaping a story, tracing the streetwalker's last night.

At a small, dark pub along the Ausschläger Allee, they

make a significant discovery. In the smoky room filled with customers who wear the cloth caps of working men, a barmaid whispers a name. Franz Seemann. She had seen him talking to the streetwalker just a few nights before the murder.

Helmuth senses Rudi's excitement, and he elbows a gentle warning to remain composed. Helmuth nods and thanks the barmaid, then nudges Rudi outside.

"I know that man," says Rudi excitedly. "He's an unemployed dockworker. He's always looking for hand-outs and a free drink. Do you think we have a suspect?"

"I don't know. We only have a name. But at least we have information for Inspector Becker, something for him to go on."

The boys hurry to the Hammer Deich station and report their findings. "Unemployed, you say?" says Inspector Becker, looking pleased. "At a time when Hitler has jobs for everyone. Sounds like a suspicious character, possibly an anarchist. There are those people who want to undermine this great country. All mentally unstable, if you ask me. In need of rehabilitation."

Helmuth's insides tighten at hearing this. He realizes something that frightens him: Inspector Becker seems to have already found Franz Seemann guilty. But Inspector Becker shakes their hands and assures them they did the right thing. He will send two agents to pick up Franz Seemann and bring him in for questioning.

Two days later, Helmuth and Rudi stop by the police station, and Inspector Becker tells them that Seemann is in prison where he belongs. Becker pumps their hands again, congratulates them for helping to solve the case, promises to keep them in mind if he has other cases for them to solve.

Helmuth pushes down the unease he feels. Surely he hasn't accused an innocent man. Surely Inspector Becker would not allow that to happen. But still the unease is there, that nagging feeling.

The next time Helmuth sees Rudi, Rudi's left arm is bandaged from wrist to elbow. "What happened?" Helmuth asks.

"An accident," says Rudi, and he tells Helmuth how he had been playing chase with other boys from his street, and how he fell through a window, shattering the glass, and severing an artery in his wrist. Rudi was rushed to the hospital for emergency surgery.

Helmuth whistles in stunned sympathy.

"That wasn't the worst part," says Rudi. "I had two visitors from the Gestapo."

"The Gestapo! What did they want?"

"To investigate me. The nurses went through my wallet and found the Lord Lister card. They reported me as a potential enemy agent!"

Helmuth snorts. "You? An enemy agent?"

Rudi snaps at Helmuth. "It's not funny. They wanted to know who Lord Lister was. Wanted to know why I worked for a British detective agency."

"Did you tell them it was a game? A made-up game?"

"Of course. But the one agent slapped me, hard. He said it was no game to them. He warned me that they take subversive activity very seriously. The second agent wanted to know if it was a cover-up for a secret underground movement."

Helmuth's insides twist. He does not want to be in trouble with the Gestapo.

Rudi looks ready to cry. "They fired question after question at me. They took my words, twisted them, and used them against me. They wanted to know what adults were involved."

"This is unfair!" says Helmuth. "A Gestapo badge is not a license to abuse innocent people."

Rudi quiets him. "I told them to ask Inspector Becker, that he would know who I am. The men wrote his name down and then said they'd check out my story, and for my sake, I'd better not be lying. I'll never forget the look in their eyes — like they enjoyed scaring me — and then they said, 'We'll find out the truth. We always do.' They took my wallet and my Lord Lister card with them."

"This is insane," says Helmuth. "We wanted to help the police and now they've turned on us."

Rudi nods. "They were trying to trip me up. Trying to get me to say something that wasn't true, trying to get me to give information about somebody else, anything at all. They wrote it all down."

"Let them take notes," says Helmuth. "All the notes they want. What do we care? We don't know anything that can hurt anyone."

"I don't ever want to go through anything like that again."

"You won't," says Helmuth. "Inspector Becker will straighten them out. That's the last you'll see of the Gestapo."

"I hope so!" says Rudi. "I felt so scared, so guilty, even though I'd done nothing wrong."

Helmuth wishes there were something more he could say, something he could do to help Rudi, but at this moment he feels helpless.

∞

Exercise time ends. The guard barks another command. Helmuth retrieves his slop bucket, trudges back to his cell. Sets the slop bucket in the corner.

It's time to clean. Helmuth takes his time, stretches out each task to pass the morning. He dusts the table, the chair, the floor, the corners, especially the corners. Dust is verboten. *Helmuth winces, doesn't want to think about the punishment that dust brings.*

As he cleans, he wonders about Franz Seemann, wonders if he was truly guilty, wonders how he held up under the Gestapo interrogation he certainly received. Helmuth knows all about Gestapo interrogations now. He knows that prisoners will say anything, admit to anything to make the torture stop. He wishes he could tell Franz Seemann how sorry he is.

Helmuth digs vigorously at the dust in the corner.

∞

The summer of 1938 turns to crisp fall. The Germans are upset at stories that Czechs and Poles are abusing ethnic Germans living in Czechoslovakia and Poland. Hitler orders troops to the border of Czechoslovakia, sending a strong warning to those who dare to mistreat Germans. He demands the Sudetenland, where many Germans live, and gets his way.

Helmuth and Rudi never hear from Inspector Becker

again. The police are too busy arresting Polish Jews living in Germany, cramming them into trains, shipping them back to Poland.

"Have you seen the long lines of Jews at the train station?" says Hugo one night in late October. "A good thing. We've got too many Jews as it is. No need to keep the Polish ones, too."

"Too many Jews?" says Gerhard. "Germany has sixty million people, and out of that sixty million, only one-half million are Jews."

"And look at the trouble those half million have caused," says Hugo matter-of-factly.

"How many Jews do you know?" asks Helmuth quietly.

Hugo thinks over his answer. "None, and now, thanks to our Führer, I will soon know even fewer." He chuckles at his own joke. "No one wants the Jews. Not even America. Americans have no right to criticize us. They rounded up their Indians, you know. Put them on reservations."

Helmuth pities the Polish Jews who are herded onto trains, shipped back to Poland, but feels sorrier still when Poland doesn't want them back. At the border, Polish authorities deny the Jews entry and detain them in open fields, without shelter, food, or water while the Polish and

German governments argue. After several tense days, the Polish government agrees to a compromise. Poland takes some of the Jews, and the rest are shipped back to Germany.

"A great victory," says Hugo. "We have shown Poland that they cannot dictate policy to us. Germany is for Germans. True Germans."

The November weather turns colder, the sky always dark and gray. Hamburg is beautiful nonetheless, with its rivers and canals, craggy spires and turrets. And for a city that had been so poor before Hitler's rise to power, the sound of work, of hammers ringing along the docks, building ships and U-boats, is beautiful, too. There's excitement in Germany. Prosperity. Pride in everything German.

But there's tension, too, and on November 7, the radio crackles with news reports about a young Jew named Herschel Grynszpan, who has shot a Nazi official, Ernst vom Rath, in Paris. A fever grips the German people as they learn that the official lies near death in a Paris hospital.

"It's a plot!" rages Hugo. "A cowardly plot! Another Jewish plot to bring Germany to its knees, to cripple the Fatherland."

"How can you call it a plot?" asks Helmuth. "It's one seventeen-year-old boy who shot one Nazi."

But Hugo won't listen. "Mark my words. It's a plot!"

The next day, to prove his point, Hugo waves the Nazi Party newspaper, the *Völkischer Beobachter*, with its thick black headlines that cry, *Outrage! World Jewry Attacks!*

"See?" he says. "I was right. And the Jews will pay for their cowardly act."

Two nights later, Mutti is clinking dinner dishes in the kitchen sink as Hugo dresses. The radio is on, has been on for two days, so Hugo can listen and sputter and shout about the news.

Hugo shrugs into his thick black coat, picks up his SS hat. He nuzzles Mutti's neck. "Be careful. Don't go out tonight," he says. "And don't wait up." There's a dangerous glint in Hugo's eyes.

Hugo leaves. Helmuth stands at the window, watches as Hugo crosses to the corner. It's drizzling. The black pavement gleams wet. The street is quiet. Oddly quiet. No police. No pedestrians. Just the distant rumble of a streetcar.

Under the gas lamp, Hugo greets several men. All are wearing uniforms. They stand proudly as if their uniforms make them something. Two are so drunk they lean against each other.

The night seems ordinary enough. Just a bit darker than usual. A bit quieter.

Mutti calls Helmuth from the window. She has changed the radio station, and a Wagner opera now fills the flat. "Come dry," she says to Helmuth, pressing a dish towel into his hand.

As Helmuth dries the last dish, the Wagner opera is interrupted. A newscaster breaks in with a special report. The Nazi official, Ernst vom Rath, has died.

After that, the night explodes. Helmuth hears distant shouts. Crashing. Splintering. The roar of engines. Trucks come and go all night.

The next morning, just as Gerhard and Helmuth finish breakfast, Hugo stumbles in the door. The smell of smoke hangs on his coat. There's a strange look of feverish excitement in his bloodshot eyes, making them a sharper and brighter blue.

Mutti brings him two soft-boiled eggs in blue eggcups and a thick slice of rye toast. Hugo grabs a knife, hatchets off the tops of his eggs. He dunks the bread in the runny yolks and gobbles it down.

Hugo turns on the radio. In full cry, the newscaster erupts with the details of spontaneous riots against the

Jews that have taken place all over Germany. It's all in retribution for the Jew who killed the Nazi official in Paris. Synagogues are burned down or nearly demolished. Jewish shops, stores, businesses, and private homes ransacked and destroyed. Jews arrested and trucked away.

"It's terrible," says Mutti. She touches Hugo's neck, folds down the collar on his shirt.

"I agree. It's not pretty," says Hugo. "People do terrible things when they're angry. But Jews must learn that they can't get away with murder."

Hugo finishes the second egg and his toast. He sucks the egg from his mustache, pushes away from the table, and heads to the bedroom. He collapses with a groan on the bed. Mutti follows him, and from the kitchen, Helmuth watches as she tugs off his boots, draws the blanket over him.

Helmuth wrestles a sudden wave of nausea as he realizes what Hugo did last night. But it's Gerhard who says something when Mutti returns. "How can you?" he whispers to Mutti. "You heard the news. How can you not say anything?"

Mutti bites her lip, doesn't answer for a long while, and when she does, she speaks without looking at her sons. "Silence is how people get on sometimes. I don't expect you to understand."

Helmuth's disgust turns to pain for his mother and disgust for himself. He recognizes silence. He's silent every night around Hugo. Every day at school when Herr Vinke says terrible things about Jews. Every meeting with the Jungvolk when they play games like "Capture the Jew."

Gerhard stalks out. Helmuth leaves, too. He heads toward school, and then changes his mind and turns toward the Grindel district. Nothing prepares him for what he sees — the work of Hugo and his Nazi friends — the ruined shops and businesses, the burned-out buildings, the smoldering synagogue, its colorful glass windows shattered; the looters, their arms heaped with clothing, shoes, everything they can carry; the splintered furniture; the weeping women pushing broken glass with their brooms. All around is misery and destruction.

Outside a pub, several drunken storm troopers sit in soot-covered uniforms, singing about the greatness of Germany. Helmuth catches the sour smell of beer, and it sickens him. He turns, catches his reflection in the window, loathes the silent German who stares back at him.

∞

Dust motes swirl in the late-morning sunlight. Helmuth follows the swirling stream to the cell window, stands on tiptoe, reaches to wipe the sill. It is verboten *to look out the window. But later he will. Later he will listen for footsteps in the corridor, the jangle of keys, and when it's clear, he will stand on the table. He will gaze beyond the high brick wall, the red-tile rooftops, the spike of church steeples, the linden and chestnut trees.*

A sparrow flits by. Nearly tempts him to the window, but he stops himself. Wants to save the best part of the afternoon for later. Doesn't want to sit, either. And so he paces. Eight steps the length of the cell. He pushes off the back wall, turns, takes eight steps back, pushes off the front wall. Back and forth, back and forth. He blocks out the jangle of keys, the clang of cell doors opening, closing, the words, "Come with us. It is time."

∞

Another Christmas. Another new year. 1939. An uneasy peace falls across Europe. That spring, Germany annexes Czechoslovakia and then demands Danzig and the Polish corridor — the land separating Germany from East Prussia. Britain and France send a stern warning to Hitler, promising to support Poland if Germany threatens to invade.

An uneasy peace settles over the Sachsenstrasse flat, too. Unable to tolerate Hugo any longer, Gerhard moves out, taking over the small bedroom in Oma and Opa's flat. Helmuth misses Gerhard and he falls into a routine designed to avoid Hugo. Morning at school. Noon meal with Oma and Opa. Evening study in his bedroom. There Helmuth also eats supper as he does his homework. At school, he takes typing and stenography classes. He prefers to practice in quiet where Hugo won't make fun. If Mutti minds that Helmuth eats alone, she doesn't say. More and more these days, silence is how they get on.

Now fourteen, Helmuth graduates into the Hitler Youth proper, though he skips the meetings as often as he dares. The Hitler Youth isn't as fun as the Jungvolk. The older boys take everything much more seriously — the drilling, the weapons training, the endless military parades. He despises their politics, too, the way they power over one another, the way might equals right. Their games are brutal, as if they enjoy shedding blood on the field, pummeling the weaker ones. And if you don't follow along, the Hitler Youth leaders threaten you with extra drills and fines and weekend detention.

Gerhard turns eighteen, and one night he and Helmuth walk down Süderstrasse, past what used to be Herr Seligmann's butcher shop and Herr Kaltenbach's bake shop. The shops now bear Aryan names and swastika banners.

"I got my letter to appear before the military induction board," Gerhard tells Helmuth.

The news stuns Helmuth. "You're being drafted? But you have school —"

Gerhard shakes his head. "They granted me a deferment until I graduate. But I must still serve six months in the Reich Labor Service."

"What about Hans?" asks Helmuth.

"He won't be drafted," says Gerhard. "He already serves the Fatherland by building submarines."

The two brothers walk on in silence. All sorts of bitter feelings rise in Helmuth until finally he says, "Hitler promises peace, but every day he moves us closer to war."

"I feel it, too," says Gerhard. "There doesn't seem to be anything we can do to stop the arrogance and hate and spite that lead to war."

Helmuth looks at the swastika banners fluttering over the shops. The flags seem to gloat, seem to goose-step triumphantly down the street.

By summer's end, the newspaper headlines scream about atrocities that Poles are committing against ethnic Germans. Hitler sends troops to the Polish border. War clouds gather and erupt.

On September 1, Helmuth bursts into his grandparents' flat and snaps on the radio. "Gerhard, did you hear?

The Poles have attacked us! They fired shots at our soldiers, and now we're firing back. We're at war!"

They listen in stunned silence. Hitler has declared war on Poland, and even now, as the RRG broadcasts the news, the Luftwaffe is bombing Poland by air, supported by tanks and infantry.

The Reich has also passed a new law, the Extraordinary Radio Law, intended to protect the Fatherland from lies and other enemy propaganda.

Gerhard turns up the volume. "Listening to foreign radio stations is forbidden," continues the newscaster. "Violations will be punished by imprisonment or by death!"

Helmuth is infuriated by this latest restriction. "How can the Nazis do this?" he asks. "How can we trust that they will tell us the truth? I love Germany, but this makes me hate it!"

"Helmuth!" says Gerhard. "Don't say such a thing! It's still our country, no matter who leads us. We must obey the law. I hate the thought of war, too, but we must defend the Fatherland, no matter what."

Helmuth snaps off the radio. The world has turned upside down — and yet it feels as though Hitler has been preparing for this moment for a very long time.

Three days later, the world spins wildly again when the British and the French honor their promise to Poland and declare war on Germany. British planes fly over Germany, littering cities with leaflets. Helmuth picks one up. It's a warning to the German people. "Your rulers have condemned you to the massacres, miseries, and privations of a war they can never hope to win," the leaflet says.

He stares at the sheet. The Nazis call these leaflets enemy propaganda, designed to undermine German morale. By law, Helmuth is supposed to destroy the leaflet, but he doesn't, not right away. How can he be expected to obey a law that feels so wrong? To obey a leader who strips away one freedom after another?

The Germans continue to strike Poland hard and fast, in a new kind of warfare called a Blitzkrieg, a lightning-fast war. Throughout September the Germans bomb cities and villages, leveling homes and buildings. There are whispers about terrible things happening in Poland, about low-flying planes that shoot women and children, about German soldiers who machine-gun Poles and Jews over mass graves. It sounds too terrible to believe.

At home, Mutti drops another kind of bomb: She and Hugo are getting married. And they do, on a Tuesday late in September.

After the short ceremony, they gather at Oma and Opa's flat. Helmuth is about to take a bite of wedding cake when Hugo says to him, "Wait and see, my boy. The war will be over, as soon as this matter is settled with Poland." With his fingers, he shoves cake into his mouth.

"It's one thing to attack a weak Poland," says Gerhard. "And quite another to take on England, the greatest power in Europe."

"Enough defeatist talk!" says Hugo. "We have to fight back. We can't let the Poles abuse Germans living in Poland!"

"What about the Nazis' atrocities?" says Helmuth. He knows he's inviting an argument, and that he shouldn't, not on Mutti's wedding day. But he can't help himself. "The Nazis don't even try to hide what they do here — to the Jews or to anyone who disagrees with them."

"Jews are not Germans," says Hugo, his temper flaring. "They are foreigners. Germany is for Germans. As for the others, we can't tolerate defeatists. They should be arrested. We must have a united front during war."

"But not at the cost of our own freedom!" says Helmuth. "Just when you think you can't lose any more freedoms, the Nazis find another to take away. Now it's against the law to listen to foreign radio."

"Such laws are necessary during wartime," says Hugo brusquely. "To protect the Fatherland. The enemy will stop at nothing to destroy our will to victory. Their propaganda caused us to lose the Great War." He fixes a stern eye on Helmuth. "What's happened to you, Helmuth? You had better watch your step or you could find yourself sitting in jail — or worse."

Helmuth feels his blood turn icy. Hugo has never called him Helmuth before, has always called him "my boy." Has he pushed Hugo too far? Has he made a mistake in revealing his true thoughts to Hugo, the Rottenführer? Would Hugo-the-good-Nazi denounce Helmuth for his beliefs?

Helmuth grows sullen and distant, unable to bring himself to eat the cake as Hugo makes small talk with Opa.

Mutti nudges Helmuth and hands him a cup of tea. A wilted mint leaf floats on top. "Hugo is not a bad person," she whispers gently.

"But, Mutti, he's wrong."

Mutti smooths Helmuth's hair into place and touches his cheek. She looks hurt.

Hugo stands, heads to the door. He nods to Mutti, his eyes warm. "Let's go," he says, crooking his arm.

Without another word to Helmuth, Mutti straightens her skirt, links her arm in Hugo's, and leaves. Helmuth looks away as the darkness spreads inside him. His mother no longer belongs to him. Mutti belongs to Hugo.

In late September, Warsaw falls. Poland surrenders, and trains filled with victorious German troops receive a jubilant homecoming.

"What did I say?" exults Hugo, clapping his hands. "The war would be over as soon as this matter with Poland is settled, and now, thanks to our Führer, it is."

Within days, however, more German soldiers are shipped on trains to the west. Throughout that fall and into the winter all of Germany holds its breath, waits for more fighting, but nothing more happens. "See?" says Hugo. "Hitler is satisfied, just as he said he would be, now that he has Poland."

Hugo is wrong.

The spring of 1940 sends German troops marching

across France. Hamburg finds itself digging the thawing ground, tearing up city parks, and building tall concrete towers armed with flak guns to shoot down enemy bombers. They also dig underground bomb shelters that can hold as many as one thousand people.

One June night, British bombers wing their way across the open water of the North Sea and grope their way up the Elbe, easily spotting Hamburg with its maze of waterways, docks, wharves, and oil refineries.

The damage is light, mostly confined to the U-boat pens and refineries, but two errant bombs land in St. Pauli, a neighborhood known for its theaters and cafes and concert halls. The first bomb hits the middle of the street, upturning the pavement and leaving a gaping hole. The second strikes a tenement, blowing away the top floors.

The next day, Helmuth and Rudi go see the damage for themselves, and it's shocking. Refuse lies everywhere. Piles of tumbled brick. Shattered floors and walls. Splintered furniture. Broken glass. Everywhere, people with shovels and pails try to clean up the mess.

"This is Hitler's fault," Helmuth tells Rudi. "He should have been satisfied with Poland, the way he said he would. But no, instead he expands the war and goes into France."

"It's revenge," says Rudi. "Hitler's getting even for the Treaty of Versailles. Germany will be humiliated no more."

Five days later, a newscaster shrills that Paris has fallen to the Germans, and the German people are overjoyed to see the Nazi flag hoisted over France. Thousands of French prisoners of war are shipped to Germany for forced labor in the German countryside, and Hitler sends the Luftwaffe to bomb Britain.

By summer's end, Gerhard leaves for mandatory Reich Labor Service, where he's stationed outside Paris, France.

"It isn't so bad," Gerhard assures Helmuth in letters. "I'm assigned to headquarters, completing paperwork. The Technicum has agreed to give me credit, so I will graduate on time. The way the war is going, who knows? I may be home sooner than we all think."

Mutti does not object when Helmuth takes over Gerhard's empty bedroom at his grandparents' flat, and soon Hans joins him. Helmuth begins working as church secretary, a volunteer position. At night, behind shuttered windows, he sits at Oma's table. He types letters on the church's Remington typewriter to fellow Mormons stationed at the front. Each keystroke, each carriage return, makes Helmuth hate Hitler and his war all the more.

One September night, Helmuth, Karl, and Rudi are walking home together from choir practice. It is growing dark, but it's not yet curfew. Helmuth begins to sing "You Are My Sunshine" in a loud voice.

It's an American song, one that the boys learned from church missionaries. The boys miss the American missionaries, who were called home when war broke out. "Come on," Helmuth urges Karl and Rudi. "Sing. You know the words."

Rudi is quiet. His English isn't very good. Karl's English isn't good, either, but that doesn't stop him. He has always loved to sing, and so he joins Helmuth in a clear voice.

Suddenly Helmuth hears the distinct sound of marching boots. Karl stops singing, but Helmuth keeps on, even more loudly as a Hitler Youth patrol rounds the corner. He's egging on the Hitler Youth, and he knows it.

"*Heil* Hitler," says the patrol leader, saluting.

Helmuth finishes the song quickly in one breath and then snaps off a smart salute. "*Heil* Hitler!" He doesn't know these boys, but he recognizes their uniforms. HJ-Streifendienst, patrol force. Junior Gestapo.

"We need to see your identification cards," says the patrol leader. The boy is Helmuth's age, with a long, lean face, sleek as a greyhound's.

"Why?" says Helmuth. "It's not curfew yet."

Rudi has his wallet out already, his identification card extracted. "Come on," he says, nudging Helmuth. "Show him your card. It's no big deal."

But to Helmuth, it is a big deal. In anger, he snaps his card out of his wallet. The leader inspects it, writes down Helmuth's name and address, hands the card back. "Guddat, why are you singing English songs?" says the leader, with an air of superiority.

"It's not English," says Helmuth, "it's American. And why shouldn't we sing it? We're not fighting Americans."

"It's un-German," says the patrol leader. "You should sing German songs. You'd better watch your step, or you'll find yourself in weekend detention and possibly even a fine."

Rudi grabs Helmuth's arm. "Come on," he says. "Let's go home."

Helmuth is seething. He throws off Rudi's hand, struggles to get himself under control. He can't afford a fine, but he wants to tell this patrol leader off.

Karl intercedes. "No need to get upset," he says to

Helmuth. And then to the patrol leader, Karl adds, "We were just having a little fun. We'll be careful and make sure our friend gets home."

"Get your friend home now," orders the patrol leader. "I'm noting this incident on my report."

The patrol force squad continues down the street and, in perfect rhythm, they pivot around the corner. Helmuth glares after them. "The Hitler Youth talk about comradeship, but what they really want to do is bully," he says, seething.

Rudi nudges Helmuth. "There are lots of things worth getting in trouble for, but not a song. Come on. Let's go home. Forget about them."

As 1940 ends, more British bombs have fallen over Hamburg, but the Nazis have overrun Poland, France, Denmark, Norway, Belgium, Luxembourg, and the Netherlands. There are rumors, too, about large camps being built in Poland, camps where Jews will be forced to work, and the German people are deliriously happy that God has given them Hitler and that God is on their side.

Helmuth, Rudi, and Brother Worbs spend New Year's Eve on air-raid duty in a cold factory building that also doubles as their church. Karl should be there, too, but he has found a New Year's party and sent a Mormon friend, Arthur Sommerfeld, as his replacement.

To pass time, Helmuth fiddles with a radio dial, trying to tune in a station other than the German Reich radio, the RRG. He twists the knob. Static. Twists again, and the radio coughs out a few garbled words of a Swiss broadcast. Twists again, and the radio growls German news.

It's frustrating. Terribly frustrating, the way the Nazis jam the airways so that the German people can only listen to broadcasts approved by the Nazis.

Helmuth longs to hear news other than the RRG, since the German news is always the same. If he lived closer to the border, he might be able to pick up a foreign station from England or Switzerland. But not here, not in Hamburg. Not with a cheap People's Radio.

Helmuth gives up on the radio, snaps it off, and turns his attention to the card game that Rudi and Arthur are playing. Brother Worbs sits off by himself in a small circle of light, reading his worn Book of Mormon.

The night passes slowly, until Brother Worbs pulls out his pocket watch and calls out, "Almost midnight, boys!"

Helmuth scrambles to his feet, out of the room, and down the hall. Rudi and Arthur follow, clambering behind, up the narrow stairs, groping their way to the rooftop. They push open the heavy door and spill out onto the roof.

In peacetime, the street lamps below would be lit and the city aglow with light. Especially tonight, New Year's Eve. People would have been heading out to parties, all dressed sharply.

Instead the night is as quiet as a shadow. Helmuth digs his hands into his pockets. He gazes at the jagged outline of buildings, at the church spires and turrets.

A car rumbles slowly down the darkened street, its headlights shrouded. The driver must be a high-ranking official, for war rationing means that only important Nazis have ample access to gas and food.

Another minute passes, and it's the new year. Where there is no light, there is suddenly noise. Church bells clang, and in the harbor, ships blare their foghorns and steam whistles shrill.

"Look," says Helmuth. The boys follow his pointing finger across the jutted rooftops where fireworks explode — blue red yellow white — a thousand points of brilliant light. It isn't as grand a celebration as it would have been before the war, but the boys gasp in amazement at the wonder and danger of it all.

"Nineteen forty-one," says Helmuth, rolling over the

feel of the numbers in his mouth, and for a moment the new year hangs there, ripe with hope and possibility.

Somewhere a police whistle shrills. There is always a fearful moment to wonder who they are coming after this time. The noise, the fireworks fade, and the boys retreat to their watch room. Brother Worbs pours hot cider, and Rudi brings out Berliners, the special jelly doughnuts that his mother has saved her ration cards to make.

Before they eat, Brother Worbs kneels and clasps his hands in prayer. In a strong voice, he prays, "Lord, give us peace, break the yoke of the Nazi butchers, make us free."

The boys are shocked into silence. They stare, open-mouthed, at Brother Worbs. He should know better. His words are dangerous and foolhardy, for Nazi informers lurk everywhere.

"You'd better watch what you say in public," whispers Rudi.

"I speak the truth," says Brother Worbs.

"You can think whatever you want," says Helmuth to Brother Worbs. "But be careful what you say."

Brother Worbs opens his Book of Mormon and continues reading, leaving the boys to check through the warehouse every few hours. Everything appears in order. The boys struggle to stay awake, but no air-raid sirens sound. Finally they fall asleep, awaking only when three Hitler Youths in uniform report for duty early the next morning.

The boys bid good-bye to Brother Worbs and walk home. Helmuth remembers the feeling of hope and possibility he felt on the rooftop. He searches for it, tries to feel it again. He feels a sudden pang of sadness and something beneath the sadness. He follows the feeling, traces it back. It's Gerhard. He misses Gerhard.

∞

Noon. The small window in the cell door slides open again. A bowl of watery cabbage soup is shoved through. The soup is possible to eat if he doesn't stop to smell it, doesn't stop to think about his grandmother's soup, her thick beef-and-barley soup, and the crusty bread to sop up the hearty broth.

He longs for a letter. He'd surely trade soup for a letter. He misses his family terribly, so terribly he aches. He knows he has caused them much sorrow, much hardship. Especially Gerhard. That he regrets, and only that.

He gulps the thin soup.

∞

The March day is bright blue as Helmuth enters the Luisenweg tenement, turns the key to the flat. The door is unlocked. Puzzled, Helmuth drops his satchel by the door, finds himself startled at a noise coming from the hall. It's Gerhard, standing at the closet, a gaping duffel bag at his feet.

"You're home!" says Helmuth.

Gerhard is a sight for sore eyes, looking strong and fit in his brown Reich Labor Service uniform. The swastika armband fits snug. He has muscled out in the seven months he's been away.

Gerhard grins. "I am. But it's only for a few days. A week, maybe two at most. Until I get my draft notice." He bends over his duffel bag and takes out a brown radio.

Helmuth spots the bright Rola logo, sucks in his breath in amazement. "A shortwave radio!" he whispers. "Where did you get it?"

Gerhard grins. "The black market," he whispers back. "Paid 5,250 francs. That's 25 marks!"

The black market. Germans stationed in France fill their duffels with items rationed or no longer available at home due to wartime restrictions. Twenty-five marks was cheap for a Rola radio — even cheaper than the People's Radio.

Gerhard sets the radio on the middle shelf in the closet. He makes room next to his paintings, his railroad cars, and his violin and mandolin and mandola. He locks everything away for safekeeping because that's the way Gerhard is.

"Wait," says Helmuth as Gerhard inserts a key in the lock. "Let me keep the radio."

"Don't be ridiculous!" says Gerhard. "You can't listen to a shortwave. You know what happens to people who break the Radio Law —" Gerhard stops midsentence, draws his finger across his throat for emphasis, makes a cutting sound.

Helmuth's temper flares. "The Führer forbids everything," he says angrily.

Helmuth holds his index finger to his upper lip, mocking Hitler's toothbrush mustache, and goose-steps across the flat. "Swing music. *Verboten*," he says. "Jitterbug dancing. *Verboten*. Reading un-German books. Singing un-German songs. Staying out past the ten o'clock curfew. Criticizing Adolf Hitler or the war. *Verboten*. *Verboten*. *Verboten*."

Gerhard grabs his brother's hand, grips it, iron-fisted. "Stop that," he whispers, shocked. "Are you a fool? Do you want the neighbors to hear?"

Gerhard relaxes his grip. "The war won't last forever. Soon the Fatherland will be victorious and then —"

Helmuth yanks his hand away, his fingers smarting. "And then what?"

"And then we will take out the radio. In the meantime, we obey the law."

Helmuth crosses to the window, pretends to watch a robin hopping about in the courtyard. There are times when he hates Gerhard. And why shouldn't he? Gerhard is so reasonable, so predictable, so resolute, always doing the right thing, obeying the law, even when he doesn't agree with it.

Gerhard stands behind him, grips Helmuth's shoulders, tries to turn Helmuth to face him. Helmuth resists. Gerhard presses harder. Helmuth gives in. Stares eye to eye with Gerhard and realizes for the first time that they are nearly the same height.

"I mean to speak to you man-to-man," says Gerhard. "Can you handle that for once?"

Helmuth winces. How Gerhard can sting with so few words.

Gerhard's eyes bore into Helmuth's. "The Nazi government is not the first unjust government in the world," he says. "Nor will it be the last. But it will come to an end."

Helmuth searches Gerhard's face. "Will it?"

"Of course it will. Everything does, at one time or another."

No, it doesn't. Not to Helmuth. The war feels like infinity. The Nazis feel like infinity.

Somewhere a police siren wails thinly, up and down, up and down, regular tempo, crisis under control, just like Gerhard. Gerhard is a good fit for the military, Helmuth decides, even though he isn't a Nazi, has never been a Nazi, has never approved of Hitler and the Nazi government.

Helmuth tries to keep the impatience out of his voice, to sound regular and even, under control like Gerhard, as if the radio doesn't matter. But his throat tightens around the words and he feels childish as he says, "Go ahead. Lock it up. See if I care."

"It's for the best," says Gerhard. "For everyone's best. To break the Radio Law would be a selfish act. It could endanger our family." Gerhard pushes the closet door tight, turns the key.

Helmuth swallows hard at the click of the lock. The sound metals every part of him, turns him cold inside. Maybe Hitler can take his rights away, but Gerhard can't. Gerhard will be gone in a few days. He can't stop Helmuth if he isn't here.

∞

It isn't a holiday, but Mutti and Oma treat Gerhard's homecoming as one. The flat is crowded with friends and family and feels as festive as Christmas. It doesn't even matter that Hugo is there, as proud of Gerhard in his smart uniform as if he were his real father.

Opa leads the family in a mealtime prayer, and then bowls and spoons are passed out. Oma ladles thick, milky potato soup, carefully scraping the bottom to find enough for all of them. Somehow there are plates of sausages, and thick, crusty bread, and even a brown cake with nuts. She cuts the cake in small pieces, enough to go around.

Helmuth is about to bite into the cake when Hugo says, "So tell us, my boy, what are you learning in school these days?"

Helmuth sets down his fork on the plate. "I'm writing my thesis for graduation," Helmuth tells him. "It's about the difference between National Socialism and a plutocracy."

"Splendid," says Hugo. "A political paper! Too bad the war will soon be over. The army could use soldiers like you. With your mind, you'd make a smashing officer. It's too bad you will have missed it."

Helmuth stops listening, feels a dark numbness spread inside. He thinks about what Mutti once said, that silence is how people get on sometimes.

With his fingers, Hugo shoves the last bite of cake into his mouth. He stands and straightens his trouser legs. "Time to go, Emma," he says to Mutti. "I'm tired, you're tired, we're all tired."

He stretches out his hand. Mutti smiles at Hugo, grasps his hand. As Helmuth watches her leave, he wonders if he'll ever understand how she could love such a man.

That night, Helmuth, Gerhard, and Hans retreat to the bedroom at Oma and Opa's flat. Hans falls asleep right away, exhausted from his day's work at the shipyards.

Helmuth lies on his back in the darkness, arms linked behind his head, watching the moon shimmer the walls. He feels like a small boy again. "Gerhard," he whispers. "Are you awake?"

"Yes."

"Do you believe God has cursed us with Hitler?"

"No," says Gerhard. "We can't blame God for Hitler. The German people gave us Hitler, when they voted Nazis into office. Like it or not, he's our Führer."

"But he's a madman. How can we support him?"

"We must support our country, especially now, in time of war, and that means supporting our leaders."

Gerhard rolls over, his back to Helmuth, conversation ended.

Helmuth lies awake for a long while, wondering if Germany deserves to win such a war.

Gerhard's homecoming ends quickly. After only two days, Gerhard receives his draft notice on bright red letterhead, ordering him to boot camp at the army camp in Reibeck-Gesthacht to the north of Hamburg.

Helmuth sits on the bed, watches Gerhard stuff undergarments and socks into his duffel bag. It doesn't feel real, watching Gerhard pack as if he's readying for a bicycle trip. He wonders if he'll see his brother again.

"I know how you feel about the war," says Gerhard. "But we must pray for Hitler to succeed, for if he does not, we all lose."

Helmuth doesn't answer, just stares at the bookshelf.

Gerhard won't let up. "Do you really think I can refuse to serve my country?"

Helmuth won't look at Gerhard; he feels childish. He knows his brother has no choice, yet he wants to blame him for that.

"You know I'm not a Nazi. But I must stand by my country," says Gerhard as he pulls the cord and makes a tight knot. "What kind of a man would I be if I didn't?"

"What kind of a man fights for something that he knows is wrong?"

Gerhard doesn't answer for a long time, and when he does, his eyes look pained. "Don't tell me that I am risking my life in vain. Don't tell me that if I die, I will have died for nothing."

Helmuth fears the answer. He swallows it and leaves the room.

That afternoon the train station is crowded with crying mothers and sweethearts, stoic fathers, and children, waving red, white, and black flags. An SA band plays. The blare of trumpets and the *rat-a-tat* of snare drums surround them. Helmuth hates the drums, hates how they quicken his blood, how they belie his true feelings and try to convince him that war is good.

Mutti cries as she stands on tiptoe, clings to Gerhard's neck, and Helmuth notices how tiny she is, how her head comes to Gerhard's nose. Gerhard lifts Mutti off the ground, kisses her, shakes Hugo's hand, and then tells Helmuth to take care of Mutti. Mutti and Oma cling to each other as Gerhard boards the train, one gray infantry soldier among hundreds of gray infantry soldiers. He pushes his way to a window, sticks out his arm, waves, shouts good-bye, his blue eyes bright with danger.

The train whistle blows, the wheels turn. Helmuth takes several deep gulps, but he can't breathe as the train pulls away.

The band picks up its tempo, and Helmuth forgets how he hates the drums, forgets how angry Gerhard can make him, remembers only that he loves his brother, remembers the nights they shared a bedroom:

Mutti tucking them in,

three brothers,

three dark heads nestled against white pillows,

white moonlight shimmering the walls,

and suddenly Helmuth is floating,

praying DearGodDearGodDearGod

keep Gerhard safe.

∞

And so prison day number 264 passes slowly, the same as every other Tuesday, until five minutes past one o'clock. It is then that Helmuth hears several footsteps outside his cell and the rattle of keys. His heart beats rapidly. He leaps to his feet, stands at attention.

Four uniformed prison officials enter his cell. They loom inside the small space, taking up all the air. Two guards accompany the officials, their hands gripping their clubs. Ready, always ready, that's what the guards are.

Helmuth barks his name, "Schutzhaftgefangener Hübener!" Prisoner Hübener! Even after all these months, Hugo's name "Hübener" feels strange in his mouth.

Six pairs of eyes study him.

"Helmuth Hübener," says one of the men.

Helmuth's heart pounds in his ears. He does not know this man, but to hear his name spoken aloud, so formally, causes his skin to tingle. This is an official visit. He knows important people have written letters on his behalf, people like his attorney and his senior district Hitler Youth leader and even Hugo, asking for clemency. He's afraid to hope, but he can't stop hope from beating inside his chest.

Helmuth nods. "Yes, sir!" he answers, his mouth as dry as sand.

"I am First State Attorney Herr Ranke," the man says. "Executory Leader." He pauses, lets his title settle over Helmuth.

The title injects Helmuth with white heat. This is the man who oversees all executions. Helmuth sways, puts his hand out to the wall to steady himself, to keep himself from melting.

Herr Ranke continues. "I am appearing by instruction from the Attorney General of the People's Court."

Helmuth straightens himself, stands tall. He looks Herr Ranke in the eye. He doesn't dare breathe, must keep hope from *flying out of his chest. He hears Herr Ranke's pocket watch. Tick. Tick. Tick. Between each tick, a thousand images flash through Helmuth's mind.*

As. Thou. wilt. As. Thou. wilt. As. Thou. wilt.

∞

Late March, 1941. Hamburg is a black pool. Windows along each street are shuttered tight and blackout shades drawn. Not a slice of light. Anywhere.

Behind a darkened window, Helmuth sits at Oma's kitchen table in a small circle of light. The table is strewn with books and papers. He reads, scribbles a few words, stares into space.

Helmuth must put the finishing touches on his final paper, his thesis required for graduation. He hates the lies he must write to get a good grade. He wishes he could write what he really thinks of Hitler and the Nazis who shipped his brother off to war.

He thinks about the Rola radio, locked in the closet for safekeeping. He glances at the clock. Five minutes until ten. He stacks his books, lines up his pencils, shuffles his papers in order. Steps softly to his grandparents' bedroom, listens at the closed door to Oma's steady breathing, Opa's light snoring. Both sound asleep. At last.

Quietly, ever so quietly, he slips a knife from the kitchen drawer, thrusts it into the hall closet lock, jabs it hard, upward, once, jimmies open the door.

The radio. Right where Gerhard left it. Helmuth whistles softly. Can't believe his good fortune, and yet he's appalled at his own rashness.

He carries the radio gingerly to the kitchen table. Turns out the light. Sits in the dark, runs his hands over the brown plastic casing. So smooth. So cool to the touch. Dare he turn it on?

He does. He twists the knob. The radio comes to life, crackling softly, a dim amber light glowing from its face. His fingers tremble. He turns the dial ever so slowly, watches the needle slide.

More crackling, and then four clear notes, *da-da-da-dummm!* Three short and one long, the first four notes of Beethoven's Fifth Symphony, the Morse code signal, V for Victory. In perfect German, the radio announcer says jauntily, as if he's announcing a tennis match, "This is BBC London with the German news broadcast!"

Helmuth's nerves jangle. His hands shake. It's the BBC, the British Broadcasting Company. Every night the BBC broadcasts a German-language edition of the news for Germans who dare to break the Radio Law.

He thinks about Gerhard, the way he locked up the

radio for safekeeping, told Helmuth to leave it alone, the way he moralized to Helmuth. *To break the Radio Law would be a selfish act. It could endanger our family.*

Gerhard irritates him all over again. "Arresting people for their beliefs is a crime," Helmuth says out loud. "Taking away our freedoms is a crime."

He leans in closer, chin on his hands. The BBC newscaster is reporting the British losses in the Atlantic. "German battleships and submarines operating in the Atlantic sank 367,800 tons of merchant vessels from March 16 through March 23," says the announcer. "The Nazis have succeeded in one of the heaviest series of blows yet claimed against British shipping."

The honesty electrifies Helmuth, the way the British announce their own losses to the Germans.

At ten-thirty, the broadcast ends. The announcer urges German listeners to find others to tune in and reminds them to turn the dial so that they won't give themselves away, if caught. Helmuth twists the dial, tunes in a Nazi-approved station, then snaps off the radio and stows it back in the closet.

Helmuth lies in bed, turning over the differences between the BBC and the RRG. The British disclose actual losses, whereas the RRG never does. It makes the British reports seem more truthful, more accurate, and that infuriates Helmuth. Don't the Germans have a right to know the whole truth?

With great relief, Helmuth finishes his final thesis, turns it in, and on the last day of school, Herr Meins stands in front of the class, grasping the graded papers. He pushes his carefully combed gray hair across his forehead. Shiny patches of scalp show, brighter and larger than when the school year began.

Helmuth often senses a sadness about Herr Meins. He can't explain it exactly, but there's something about his eyes, their reaction when the class discusses National Socialism, as if Herr Meins isn't really a Nazi at heart but does not dare say so.

"I have your final papers here," says Herr Meins, waving the sheath of papers.

Helmuth's classmates shift uncomfortably in their seats and tug at their neck collars, eager for dismissal.

Herr Meins licks his lips, the way he does when he's searching for the exact words he wants to say. He's never in a hurry to dismiss his students; he always wants to impart one more bit of knowledge before he sends them into the world.

"Each one of you has a gift," he begins. "Something you can offer the Fatherland." He looks at their faces as if he can predict what will become of them, and in one sense he can, since teachers write thorough notations in their students' Party record books. Notations that will follow them throughout their lives.

"Some of you are gifted in mathematics," he says. "Some in science, some in sports, some in leadership. And yet, as different as each of your gifts is, together you form one body, an intricate part of one machine."

The boys fidget, try to keep their eyes from the clock. Herr Meins clears his throat, snaps each squirming boy back to attention. "One paper stands out from the rest. It is written by a young man who has the gift of interpretation."

He plucks the top paper from the stack. "'The War of the Plutocrats,'" he reads.

Helmuth feels his face redden. It's his paper.

"This essay suits the ideals of National Socialism," explains Herr Meins in a faltering voice. "A plutocracy is a selfish government controlled by the wealthy. But National Socialism is a selfless government. A good Nazi works for the good of the Fatherland, not for self-interest and self-gain. A good Nazi is a good soldier for the Fatherland, one who can lead as well as follow."

For a brief second, their eyes meet, and in that brief second, Helmuth sees a flicker in his teacher's eyes.

Helmuth wonders if Herr Meins believes his own words about National Socialism.

"This paper was written by a student advanced in his years," continues Herr Meins. He returns Helmuth's paper to the stack and sets the stack on his desk. "These papers will become part of your permanent record," he says.

Herr Meins glances up at the clock. "Helmuth, please remain. The rest of you are dismissed. *Heil* Hitler!"

Helmuth wonders what his teacher wants as his classmates rush for the door. Perhaps Herr Meins has thoughts like Helmuth, thoughts he cannot dare to write. Perhaps that is what Herr Meins wants to tell him. Helmuth's hands tremble with anticipation.

The room is empty, quiet. Herr Meins sits in a student desk next to Helmuth. Folds his hands on his lap. "You will go far," he says to Helmuth. "Your essay shows that a leader can lead with words as well as action." Then he adds softly, "But in class, your idealism shows as well. Be careful of idealism, my boy, for idealism is the most dangerous doctrine of all." And there it is again. The flicker.

Helmuth nurses a desire to blurt out the truth that his paper is a lie, that it turned his stomach to write it and that he never will write such lies again, now that he has earned his Oberbau diploma. He senses that Herr Meins would understand. But then, the flicker is snuffed out, and in its place, hardness, and so Helmuth says, "I will go far. Just you wait and see. Some day you will hear something great about me."

Helmuth graduates, and May finds him working at the Bieberhaus, the social welfare department at the City Hall. It's a coveted apprenticeship, one awarded to those who excel in school and are expected to move into important government positions.

Hugo is proud. "With your head, the government can use you," Hugo tells him.

Soon Helmuth knows his way around the administrative offices, and one morning he's sent to file papers in a basement storeroom. He swings open the storeroom door and gropes for the light switch. The single overhead bulb floods the room, and he blinks in amazement. From floor to ceiling he sees books, rows and rows of books.

In amazement, he trails his finger across the dusty spines, reads the names of forbidden authors such as Thomas Mann and his brother Heinrich Mann, the Jewish writer Heinrich Heine, the author Erich Maria Remarque, the philosopher Karl Marx, the American author Jack London, and more. Helmuth feels stunned. He thought these books had all been burned eight years earlier. But here they are, in the dusty storeroom beneath City Hall.

He plucks a book from the shelf, *Geist und Tat, Spirit and Action,* by Heinrich Mann, who criticized Germany's growing fascism so loudly that he was forced to flee after Hitler became chancellor.

Helmuth hesitates. He knows the risk reading such a book would pose. It could get him fired, or worse, cause serious trouble for his family. He starts to wedge the book back in its place, but stops, holds it in both hands, as if weighing it. Why are the Nazis so afraid of words? What don't they want him to know?

Helmuth can't explain it, but reading that book feels necessary, as necessary as breath. He won't be caught, not if he's careful. Helmuth slips the book beneath his shirt, shuts off the light, eases the door closed, returns upstairs to his desk.

Helmuth glances at the other apprentices — Gerhard Düwer, Werner Kranz — and at his boss, Heinrich Mohns, who is at the office Betriebsobmann. It's Herr Mohns's job to ensure that all employees are loyal Nazis.

They are all bent busily over their desks. Helmuth's heart beats wildly as he sits at his desk and slides the book from his shirt into his satchel. No one suspects a thing.

Several nights later Oma and Opa are sitting on the couch, listening to the RRG, when Rudi visits after supper. Helmuth beckons him into his bedroom and closes the door. He reaches beneath his mattress, takes out the Heinrich Mann book, and shows him.

"Heinrich Mann! Where did you get that?" whispers Rudi.

"At work," says Helmuth in an excited whisper. "There's a whole storeroom filled with forbidden books. Rows and rows of them."

Rudi backs away. "You're crazy," he says. "Do you know how much trouble you can get in? If the Gestapo catch you stealing books — "

"I didn't steal it. I borrowed it. And the Gestapo have better things to do than catch me." Helmuth thumbs through *Geist und Tat*, stops at a page he has lightly outlined with pencil. "Listen to this. Heinrich Mann says that revolutions are rare because people are too selfish. They think only of themselves."

Rudi looks at Helmuth incredulously. "You want to start a revolution?"

"Think about it — if more Germans spoke out, leaders like Hitler wouldn't be allowed to lie and say 'I want peace' and then start a war." Helmuth jabs at the page with his forefinger. "The French knew how to overthrow oppression and tyranny. We could learn a lot from the French."

"Helmuth!" says Rudi, shocked. "You could get arrested for saying those things."

Helmuth continues to flip through the book. "Just look at the French Revolution! Look at their motto — Equality, Liberty, Fraternity. That was their battle cry! Those are things we've given up, that the Nazis have taken from us."

Rudi's face folds into worry. "What is it that you want, Helmuth?"

Helmuth sits, closes his eyes. Takes a deep breath. Feels a warm calm fill him, and suddenly knows. He opens his eyes. *"Geist und Tat,"* he says. Spirit and Action. That's what Helmuth wants.

By June, it seems as though Hitler can do no wrong. The Nazis have overrun Greece and Yugoslavia. Some countries join the Germans: Yugoslavia, Greece, Bulgaria, Italy, and Romania. One Saturday night, Helmuth is eating dinner with Mutti and Hugo — a rare occurrence since Helmuth has moved in with his grandparents. Helmuth spears a potato dumpling with his fork when

Hugo says, "Have you heard your old friend Heinrich Worbs has been arrested?"

"Arrested! For what?"

"That old fool," says Hugo. "Doesn't know enough to keep his mouth shut, to keep his opinions to himself. He spouted off about a Nazi statue!"

"What did he say?" asks Mutti, clearly worried.

Hugo shakes his head in disbelief. "'Another Nazi butcher that we must salute.' That's what he said. What does he think he's going to gain? He knows the law."

"How could they arrest an old man?" says Mutti.

Hugo pounds the table with his fist. "We're at war! We can't permit such defeatist talk. Complainers and grumblers, doubters and agitators — they only serve to embolden the enemy."

Mutti grows quiet. Helmuth pushes himself away from the table, doesn't feel like eating. He leaves the flat, doesn't feel like going home to his grandparents. He walks along the River Bille and watches the water sweeping past.

His head throbs with sorrow and anger and disgust. It's just as Heinrich Mann said, no one is willing to go against the current, to take a stand. Life is too short to think about others.

The next day, Helmuth finds Rudi and Karl before church. "I have terrible news," says Helmuth. "The Gestapo arrested Brother Worbs!"

"Heinrich Worbs?" says Karl. "Why?"

Helmuth tells them what Hugo had said, that Brother Worbs was denounced by someone who heard him criticize the Nazis, and now he was taken into protective custody.

"Protective custody," says Karl sarcastically. "And where are they protecting him?"

"Neuengamme," says Helmuth.

"Not a place for a sixty-six-year-old man," says Rudi, his voice filled with sympathy.

It is well known that Neuengamme is a concentration camp near Hamburg, notorious for its subhuman conditions, where brutal guards force prisoners to do hard labor with inadequate food and live in squalid cells.

"We have no one to blame but ourselves," says Helmuth. "The Nazis tell us what to think, what to feel. They tell us to hate and we call it love. They tell us to denounce our neighbors and we call it patriotism."

"But look what they do to people who dare to challenge them," says Karl. "They crush dissent, any way they can."

It's June 22, 1941, a hot summer day, and the boys meet after work at the community swimming pool at Ohlsdorf. They shake out their towels, spread them on the grass. Through loudspeakers surrounding the pool, a Schubert sonata plays, violins and cellos.

Karl and Rudi are discussing Hitler's closest friend and third-highest Nazi, Rudolf Hess, who has been missing for several weeks. The Nazis claim that Comrade Hess met with an accident over the North Sea while piloting a fighter plane.

"The Führer says Hess was deranged, in no condition to fly," says Karl. "Apparently he's been suffering hallucinations."

"Do you think he's dead?" asks Rudi.

"He's not deranged or dead," says Helmuth without thinking. "He's sitting in a British jail."

Rudi and Karl move closer. "How do you know that?" asks Rudi.

Helmuth realizes he's given himself away. The BBC announced Hess's desertion weeks ago. Hess had commandeered a fighter plane and landed in Glasgow, Scotland, where he was captured. The BBC called it the greatest escape in history.

Helmuth toys with the idea of telling his friends the

truth. He knows he can trust them. But he doesn't get the chance to answer. Suddenly the music stops, interrupted by a strident-voiced announcer.

"*Achtung!*" says the newscaster. "Attention! At four-fifteen this morning, German troops crossed the Soviet border and our Luftwaffe began to bomb Soviet naval and air bases, destroying one-quarter of the Russian air force. At six A.M. the Führer declared war on Russia!"

There's a flare of military music, and then Adolf Hitler's voice comes over the radio. "German people!" shouts Hitler. "At this moment, an attack unprecedented in the history of the world in its extent and size has begun. The purpose of this front is no longer the protection of the individual nation, but the safety of Europe, and therefore the salvation of everyone. May God help us in this battle."

All around, men, women, and children freeze in their places, stone still. Their faces are worried. They swallow hard, speak in hushed whispers.

"Now we're fighting the British and the Russians!" says Karl.

"This will take double the troops and military supplies," whispers Helmuth. "Every day that Germans spend at the Russian front will be a gain for the British."

"But we've got the best army in the world," says Rudi. "And if Hitler wins Russia, think of what it will give him — Russian airplanes and tanks and guns —"

But Helmuth knows different. "No one in history has ever conquered the Russians. Now how many more people will have to die?"

On the RRG Helmuth hears how the advancing Germans capture or kill great numbers of Russian soldiers. But the RRG never lists German losses. And so, for the truth, Helmuth tunes in to the BBC. Late each night, he opens the hall closet and takes out the Rola radio. He locks the flat door, and then hears a different story: about German planes destroyed by the Russians, sunken transport ships, and soldiers killed or captured. The Russians are fighting bitterly and bravely, but only Helmuth seems to know.

When the BBC broadcast ends, he has trouble falling asleep. The BBC keys him up, makes him hate Hitler and the Nazis and their secrets and lies all the more. Makes him ache with worry for Gerhard.

Some mornings, Oma comments on the dark circles under Helmuth's eyes. She presses her hand against his forehead to check for fever.

"Are you getting enough sleep?" she asks.

"I'm fine, Oma," he says. "There's nothing to worry about."

But he knows plenty that worries him, and one warm August night, as Helmuth walks with Karl along the Bille, their talk turns to the war in Russia. The German people have been asked to donate woolen and fur clothing for the soldiers at the Russian front, where winter comes early.

"All the fur and woolen clothing can't prepare our soldiers for winter in Russia," says Karl.

"Our luck can't hold," says Helmuth. "No army has ever won Russia, not even Frederick the Great or Napoleon."

"If we stop now, we'd have Austria, the Sudetenland, and Poland," says Karl. "Isn't that enough?"

"Europe isn't enough for Hitler," Helmuth says bitterly. "Hitler believes that world peace can only come through German domination."

The two friends walk on in silence. The secrets Helmuth keeps to himself weigh heavier with each step. He thinks of Heinrich Mann and feels selfish. God gave him the ability to think for himself — and yet he fears doing what he knows is right. He longs to share the truth with Karl.

"You know what I think?" he says to Karl.

"I'm afraid to ask," answers Karl.

Helmuth lowers his voice. "Our government is lying to us. That's what I think."

Karl winces and draws away. "It's dangerous to think that much," he says.

"Freedom has always been dangerous," says Helmuth. "Come to my place tonight, and I'll prove the Nazis are lying. But wait until after nine, after my grandparents go to bed."

After a frugal supper of cabbage-and-carrot soup and *Leberwurst*, liver sausage, Helmuth hurries Oma as they clear away the dishes. Finally Oma and Opa retreat to their bedroom and latch the door behind them.

Helmuth paces the living room and listens for footsteps. At last he hears feet shuffle outside the flat. Before Karl has a chance to knock, Helmuth swings open the door. He ushers him in, his finger to his lips, signaling for quiet.

"So what is it?" whispers Karl. "What sort of proof do you have?"

"You'll see," says Helmuth.

He eases open the closet, takes out the Rola shortwave radio, sets it on the kitchen table, directly in front of Karl.

Karl swallows hard. "Are you crazy?" He gingerly touches the raised Rola lettering, as if afraid it will shock him, but then his eyes shine with interest. "What can you hear on it?"

"You'll see," says Helmuth as he rigs up the wire antenna. He turns out the kitchen light, snaps on the radio. The radio hums to life; its dim amber light casts an eerie glow in the darkness.

Helmuth turns the dial. The radio crackles and squawks, interrupted now and then by a soothing French voice, then a wisp of violin and a quiet French horn. And then the first four notes of Beethoven's Fifth Symphony crackle from the speaker, followed by an announcer who says in crisp German, "The BBC London presents the news in German."

Karl bolts upright. "That's England!"

Helmuth gives Karl a triumphant look. "Settle down," he says. "You don't want to wake my grandparents." He adjusts the volume.

"What if someone hears us?" says Karl.

Helmuth hears the nervousness edging Karl's voice. He nods toward the flat door and tells Karl, "You don't have to stay if you're afraid."

Karl shakes his head, settles himself firmly in the chair. "I'm not afraid," he says.

"Good," says Helmuth, but he understands Karl's fear. His own heart pounds each time he listens to the BBC. It is every good German's duty to report enemy propaganda to the Gestapo, to turn in anyone suspected of listening to or reading enemy propaganda. Helmuth tries not to think about the danger.

The news that night is all about the Russian campaign. It's nothing like the German reports. All week long the RRG had boasted of great successes in Russia, one battle victory after another, with little or no German losses as the German army advanced on Smolensk.

But the BBC tells a different story.

"The Germans approached within rifle range," recounts the BBC broadcaster. "Then the Russians opened up with grenades and machine guns. The Russians organized a bayonet counterattack and forced the Germans to retreat. The Nazis left behind twenty-five hundred dead and wounded, thirty tanks and Bren Gun Carriers, eighty motorcycles, almost five hundred automatic weapons, ninety machine guns, and forty-five mortars."

Karl looks sickened. "A bayonet charge!"

Helmuth feels sickened, too. He can't bear to think what Gerhard might face if he's sent to Russia.

"Do you think the BBC is telling the truth?" asks Karl.

Helmuth nods. "The BBC reports give more details. They give their own casualties, too, not just ours. They don't hide the news from the British people. They just give the information, without telling us how to interpret it." He looks at Karl. "I despise the Nazis. I hate the way they bully people. I hate the way they lie to us. And I hate them telling me what to think."

"But what can we do? Look what happens when people speak out! They're arrested. Taken to camps. Some are never seen again. Look what they did to Brother Worbs!"

"I hate myself for doing nothing," says Helmuth bitterly. "For allowing this to happen. Everyone craves security. But gaining freedom means losing security."

"You sound like a bloody pamphlet," says Karl.

Helmuth likes that. "Do you want to listen again tomorrow?" he asks.

Karl grimaces, looks sheepish. "My parents won't let me out every night. They're afraid I'll get caught in an air raid."

Helmuth knows Karl's parents are strict about curfew, especially his father. But he also senses his friend's fear of breaking the law.

Karl leaves and Helmuth sits back at the table, presses his back against the chair. He twists the dial to the RRG, and as he listens, he grows angry all over again at its twisted lies.

Suddenly Karl's face floats in front of Helmuth. *You sound like a bloody pamphlet.*

You sound like a bloody pamphlet.

A bloody pamphlet.

A pamphlet.

Helmuth feels his thoughts changing, charging ahead to a dangerous place. Slowly an idea rises to the surface, floats in front of Helmuth. He catches it, breathes it in, and it grips him, won't let him go.

He snaps on the light, takes out a piece of paper, jots down everything he can remember from the BBC broadcast. By midnight he has an essay, titled, "Who Is Lying?"

The next night Helmuth invites Rudi to listen to the radio. He doesn't mention that Karl listened the night before. It's safer that way.

As soon as the announcer says, "This is BBC London," Rudi nearly knocks over his chair. "That's a shortwave!" he cries. "What if someone hears?"

"No one will hear if you keep your voice down," says Helmuth. "I've been listening for weeks now and I'm still here."

Rudi looks unconvinced. "But it's against the law!"

"I won't force you to stay," says Helmuth. "You can leave now and never come back. Maybe someday you will find some courage."

The words sting, Helmuth knows. He regrets hurting Rudi's feelings, but he tells himself that the words are for Rudi's own good.

Rudi plants himself solidly in his chair. "I'm staying."

"It's fine," Helmuth assures him. "You want to know the truth, don't you?"

Throughout August, Helmuth listens to the BBC, one night with Karl and another night with Rudi. He feels guilty over this deception, but he knows it's best to meet separately, for their own sake as well as his.

They sit in the dark, the small flat lit only by the dim amber light of the radio, and listen to the British voices pulsing across the crackling airwaves. It's thrilling, too, to know they're breaking the Nazi law. Breaking the law goes against their church teachings, but the boys feel sure that they have a responsibility to learn the truth.

September. Helmuth decides it's time to bring Karl and Rudi together, so they can all listen to the BBC. As he waits for Karl one night, he grows impatient. Usually Karl is right on time, but tonight he's late.

At last, at the familiar knock, Helmuth flings open the door. "Where have you been?" he asks.

Helmuth doesn't wait for Karl to answer. He beckons him inside. At the kitchen table sits Rudi. The two boys stare in shock at each other and then in betrayal at Helmuth.

Helmuth ushers them outside, saying, "Let's get some fresh air. I'll explain everything."

Outside Karl paces back and forth, angry. "Why the secrecy, Helmuth? Didn't you think you could trust us?"

"Of course I trust you!" says Helmuth. "It was for your own protection, your own safety —"

"Safety!" says Karl. "That's what the Nazis say when they keep the truth from us."

"It's not the same thing," says Helmuth. "Suppose the Gestapo arrested you or Rudi, suppose they questioned you. You know they'll stop at nothing to get names. This way, you only knew one name, mine."

Fear flashes across Rudi's face. "He's right, Karl. Remember what happened to me in the hospital?"

"But Helmuth wasn't honest with us!" says Karl. "We had a right to know. We're not Nazis."

The words sting, but Helmuth knows that Karl is right — even if Helmuth's intentions were good. "I'm sorry," he says. "I didn't mean to hurt your feelings."

Karl lets the apology settle over him. "All right," he says. "It's nearly ten o'clock. Let's go inside."

And just like that, the tension is lifted as the three friends head inside.

In the kitchen Helmuth tries to tune in London. The radio bleeps and buzzes and squawks and crackles so much that it's impossible to hear a word. He waits a few minutes, tries again, turning the dial this way and that, but no use. The jamming is too strong.

"Maybe it's for the best," says Rudi. He stands, looks anxious to leave. Karl stands, too.

Helmuth remains seated. He looks at his friends. "Wait. There's another reason why I brought you together tonight. I want you both to know that I've decided to serve the Fatherland."

Karl and Rudi look at Helmuth uneasily. "What do you mean?" says Karl.

Helmuth goes into his bedroom. He returns with his carefully written notes and a short stack of handwritten leaflets. He hands one to Karl, who reads out loud, " 'It's All Hitler's Fault!' "

Karl looks at Helmuth in disbelief, continues reading. "'During the unrestricted air raids, several hundred thousand defenseless civilians were killed. The British Royal Air Force is not to blame for these killings. Their flights are retaliation for those killed by the German Luftwaffe in Warsaw and Rotterdam. The Luftwaffe murdered defenseless women and children, cripples and old men.'"

"Are you crazy?" says Rudi.

"I've got more," says Helmuth. He pages through the leaflets, reads off others that he's written: "Hitler the Murderer," "They're Not Telling You Everything!" "Where Is Rudolf Hess?" and "Hitler Youth."

Rudi grabs the Hitler Youth flier. "'German boys,'" he reads. "'Do you know what the Hitler Youth is and what goals it pursues?'" Rudi grunts in agreement. "'It's a compulsory organization of the highest order for the cultivation of obedient Nazis.'"

"You sure got that right," says Karl. "These fliers are really something, the way you attack the Nazis."

Helmuth looks earnestly at his friends. "We must attack. We're being lied to. We must let people know the truth. Read the last line, Karl."

"'This is a chain letter, so please pass it on!'" reads Karl.

"This is a war against lies," says Helmuth. "If we want to win, we can't attack in straight lines. We'll leave leaflets everywhere — in telephone booths, mailboxes, apartment houses — for people to read and to pass on, like a chain letter!"

"They'll pass them on, all right. Right to the Gestapo," says Karl.

"Helmuth," says Rudi. "Remember our Lord Lister ID cards? How quickly they were passed to the Gestapo? And this is worse — it's no game."

"Of course it's no game! Every day the newspaper tells us about people who are sentenced to death or prison for breaking the Radio Law when all they want is the truth. This is serious."

"Do you really think we can fight the Nazi government?" says Karl. "They're too big, too powerful."

"We must fight — with words and actions. Not everyone agrees with Hitler and the Nazi Party," says Helmuth. "If we tell the real story about the war, show people that they're not alone, they will start to talk. Then they will grow in strength and numbers."

"What if the Gestapo catches us?" asks Karl. "It's serious to break the law like this."

"This kind of law must be broken. And besides, the Gestapo will never catch us," says Helmuth. "We'll make sure they don't. They might find the leaflets, but they won't know who did it. And they'll never suspect kids."

"But what if they do?" says Rudi.

Helmuth considers the possibility. "Then that person should take all the blame," he says decidedly.

Rudi's eyes widen. He looks at Karl.

"We're all under eighteen," says Helmuth. "Even if we are caught, we won't be tried as adults." He stares at the pamphlets. "I don't want to remember a time I could have done something but didn't."

The boys are silent for a long moment. "You're right," says Karl, sticking out his hand. "Count me in. No names."

"No names," says Rudi.

"No names," says Helmuth.

The boys pump each other's hands vigorously. Helmuth takes half the pamphlets, divides the rest between Karl and Rudi.

Outside the flat, on the street, Helmuth watches as Karl and Rudi head down the street. The sky looks like gray wool, and that's a good thing. The cloud cover will keep British bombers away. Helmuth heads in the opposite direction, down Luisenweg, leaflets tucked beneath his shirt.

***

October comes. The German army continues its advance on Leningrad. Gerhard graduates from training in the signal corps and is sent to officer training school in Warsaw.

That news makes Hugo as proud of Gerhard as if he were his own son. "See, Emma?" says Hugo. "I told you he'd come around."

It irritates Helmuth. He knows Gerhard is no Nazi — even if he is a soldier.

Hugo adopts Helmuth. His relationship with Hugo has not improved, but Helmuth knows having Hugo's last name, Hübener, will have its benefits. No one would ever suspect that the son of a Rottenführer would resist the Nazis. At work, at home, Helmuth is a good Nazi — smooth and unruffled on the surface but paddling furiously beneath.

As the leaves change color and drop, it gets so the boys can hardly wait from one weekend to the next — for the Friday and Saturday nights when they turn off the kitchen light and sit in the dark, listening to the BBC.

From his church Helmuth helps himself to carbon paper and typing paper — bright red paper, rarely used, so it won't be missed. He knows it's wrong to steal from the church, but he tells himself it's for the greater good, it's a war for truth that he's waging.

Late into the night in his grandparents' flat, Helmuth pecks away at the old Remington typewriter keys. Oma grows accustomed to the incessant tapping, the constant ring of the carriage return. She never asks what he's doing, or if he's getting enough sleep. Instead, she says, "My, what a hard worker you are. Your boss must be pleased."

At first Helmuth prepares new leaflets every two weeks and then every week, and then twice a week. At night, the boys leave them in telephone booths, mailboxes, even tacked to bulletin boards in tenement hallways, right next to official Nazi government notices announcing meetings such as "Tomorrow: Home Evening with Party Comrade to Discuss Air Raid Wardens."

As time goes on, the boys feel new confidence at how easily their plan is working.

From work, Helmuth borrows an official swastika stamper that makes each flier look like an official government notice, and his grandmother gets used to the constant *thump-thump* she hears each night at the kitchen table.

The stamper is a brazen touch, but it's Karl who astounds Helmuth and Rudi with the risks he takes.

Once Karl tucked fliers into coat pockets in a cloak-room. The coats — he could tell from their medals and insignia — belonged to high Nazi officials.

But Karl has a close call one night when he meets two policemen near his flat. He manages to greet the two men with a forceful "*Heil* Hitler." The policemen question him, demand to know why he is out past curfew. But Karl explains he was visiting a friend in Reismühle. The offi-cers let him go with a warning.

Karl goes straight home, rushes to the toilet, his hands shaking so badly he can barely unzip his trousers.

"Those blasted leaflets gave me the trots," he tells the boys the next night, and hearing that, Helmuth and Rudi clutch their stomachs and laugh until the tears roll down their cheeks.

It would have been easy to leave their leaflet cam-paign at that, at mailboxes and telephone booths and ten-ement hallways — but the war takes a dark, unexpected turn in early December when the Japanese bomb Pearl Harbor.

America declares war on Japan, and Germany declares war on America. This makes Hugo crabby and sour. "Roosevelt has his war now," he says. "Thanks to his

Jewish advisors. It's all the Jews' fault, you know. All part of their plan to destroy the German Reich."

But just as quickly, Hugo catches himself and his gloom disappears. "We've got the best army in the world. Someday, after we've beaten them, we'll visit America, my boy. We'll see that Wild West you like so much!"

And then something else happens that agitates Helmuth, that makes him all the more determined to wake up the people of Germany.

Brother Worbs returns.

It's late December, and the morning light is gray as Helmuth heads to the Bieberhaus, intent on returning a "borrowed" book to the City Hall storeroom before his boss, Heinrich Mohns, arrives.

He passes an old Jewish woman pushing a broom in the street. She wears a yellow star pinned to her frayed brown coat. Like a bright yellow flame. All the Jews wear stars now, so Germans can keep an eye on them.

Helmuth nearly passes by a small, stooped figure shuffling down the sidewalk. Were it not for his profile, his familiar sharp nose, Helmuth would not have recognized the old man. It's Brother Worbs.

Helmuth puts his hand on the man's arm. How thin the bony arm feels beneath the coat sleeve. Brother Worbs tugs his arm away in fright, gazes through watery eyes at Helmuth. His face is gray.

"Brother Worbs! It's me! Helmuth!"

Brother Worbs wipes his eyes with the back of his hand, tries to pull his arm away. "Let me go. It's better for you if you don't know me. Better for all of us."

That's when Helmuth sees that Brother Worbs has no teeth. His lips wreathe about swollen gums.

"My God, what did they do to you?"

Brother Worbs sways unsteadily. "Don't ask. I cannot tell you."

Helmuth decides to return the book later, at lunch, perhaps, or when he's sent on another errand to file papers. He grasps the man's elbow, guides him home, helps him off with his coat, hangs it on the hook behind the door. Brother Worbs's flat is a mess: dirty dishes, clothes lying around, drawers pulled open.

Helmuth helps Brother Worbs to a chair, puts the kettle on, clears a spot at the kitchen table, sets out a chipped teacup, finds peppermint leaves, pinches them into the teapot.

The kettle boils. Helmuth pours the water over the leaves, lets the peppermint steep. Brother Worbs's hands tremble as he reaches for the cup. His hands are gnarled, his fingers thick and crooked. "Your hands!" says Helmuth. "What happened?"

Brother Worbs looks fearful. "The SS made me sign a paper. I can only tell you that I was treated well."

"You must tell me," urges Helmuth.

Brother Worbs lowers his voice to a whisper. Tells Helmuth about the concentration camp, about the starvation rations, the guards, the punishments, how he was stripped naked, forced to stand outside, knee deep in snow, how the guards poured water on his hands, let them freeze, and then hit his hands with a club. "To warm them up," he says. "Broke all my fingers."

Helmuth touches the rough skin, the twisted fingers. Never has he witnessed such inhumanity. Fury burns inside him as he imagines the old man's pain. "The Nazis are monsters. How can they get away with torture?"

"The Gestapo are above the law," says Brother Worbs. "Whatever the Führer wants is legal, no matter how inhumane. Hitler himself says so. When the Gestapo question you, you'll admit to anything just to get the pain to stop."

"They're monstrous bullies!" says Helmuth. "The way they terrorize the weak! Surely there's something we can do!"

"We must pray for those who hate and persecute us," says Brother Worbs.

"Pray for them! That's impossible! I hate them!"

"You cannot repay evil with evil," says Brother Worbs. "God loves us all. He does not love us more than He loves our enemies."

He takes in the old man's stooped shoulders, the pain behind his eyes. Gone is Brother Worbs's spirit, gone is the old man that Helmuth loved, shouts and all, and in his place, a broken man.

Helmuth wishes he could stay longer but knows his boss will ask questions. He stands, slips his arm around the man's thin shoulders. "God bless, Brother Worbs. I'll visit you again soon."

"It's best if you don't visit me."

Helmuth plunges his arms through his coat sleeves, jams his hat on his head. He flings his arms as his feet pound the sidewalk. With each step, he sees images of Brother Worbs's hands.

By the time Helmuth reaches the Bieberhaus and returns the borrowed book, the words to another pamphlet have formed in his head. He carries the words with him all day, letting them sort themselves into phrases, coming together, drifting apart, tumbling over onto themselves, settling into sentences, and paragraphs.

That night as soon as the supper dishes are cleared, and Oma and Opa are safely in bed, Helmuth sets out the typewriter. He inserts carbon paper into the carriage and rolls it into place. Brother Worbs, his toothless gums and his gnarled fingers; soldiers dying in Russia; his grandparents and neighbors hunkered in air-raid shelters as bombs fall; burned-out Jewish businesses and synagogues; the lies, deception — he can't shake the images, his anger. He must be willing to give up safety and comfort for freedom. That's what Heinrich Mann said.

Helmuth's fingers fly over the keys, and by midnight he has a stack of new leaflets. He expects to feel satisfied but doesn't.

The Nazis can't get away with these things. The world has gone mad! It's time to think bigger, to escalate the pamphlet campaign, to enlarge his circle so that more Germans learn the truth. There's no time to lose. What will the Nazis do next if no one stops them now?

Another Christmas comes and goes and the holiday feels gloomier than ever. Karl's away, visiting an aunt who lives on a farm in Ludelsen in order to bring home food for his family. In the city, food rations have grown more meager. Coupons are needed for everything, from flour to shoes, and yet the Nazis continue to press for war donations — more woolen clothing for the soldiers and German marks to buy cannons, tanks, and airplanes.

Helmuth attends a church dance on New Year's Eve but doesn't enjoy himself. All he can think about is the war and his pamphlets. Dances feel like a waste of time. He can't afford to lose time.

Still he must practice caution. At work, he grows friendly with another apprentice, Gerhard Düwer, who rolls his eyes at the reports on the RRG when the Nazis announce that over seventy million woolen articles have been collected for soldiers on the eastern front.

"And yet our soldiers are still freezing," says Düwer disgustedly.

Helmuth is delighted at this sign, and he invites Düwer home to listen to the BBC. Düwer is enthusiastic about Helmuth's shortwave radio, and he asks to listen again.

After several more visits, Helmuth grows more sure of Düwer. He shows him his latest pamphlet, titled, "I've Figured Out Everything."

Düwer reads the pamphlet aloud. "'It's been one month since the German radio and newspapers boasted the results of the clothing drive. Over seventy million articles of clothing! But where is this clothing? The soldiers on the eastern front and the soldiers in the far north haven't received them. They do not write home about it, only that they are freezing, freezing, and freezing, and they are waiting in vain for warm winter clothes.'"

Düwer grins at the last sentence. " 'Only time will tell if the Nazis have swindled the German people out of their woolen and furs.' " He looks at Helmuth. "This is amazing. Whoever wrote this has the guts to say what everyone is thinking."

"I wrote it," says Helmuth proudly. "It's a chain letter."

Düwer whistles softly, looks at Helmuth with keen admiration. "Listen," he says in a low voice. "I know two printing apprentices in Kiel. They can be trusted to print pamphlets — hundreds of pamphlets — after hours."

Helmuth can scarcely believe his good fortune. A printing press! His mind dances with the thought of hundreds — maybe thousands — of leaflets scattered throughout Germany.

A few days later in January, another good sign comes during a class for Bieberhaus apprentices. Helmuth spots Werner Kranz jotting down French vocabulary words and grows curious. He wonders why Werner is so interested in the French. Perhaps Werner feels sympathy for the two million French prisoners of war that the Nazis have forced into labor in Germany. It's no secret that the French hate Hitler, for what he has done to their country.

An idea takes root. If Werner will translate the leaflets into French, perhaps Helmuth could smuggle them to the French prisoners. From there, the leaflets may get into the hands of the French resistance. This way the French and perhaps the whole world will learn that many Germans don't support Hitler and the war. It's a bold move, Helmuth knows. But he has heard about a group of Communists working underground who have connections.

Helmuth approaches Werner Kranz quietly. "Would you translate something into French for me?"

"It depends on what it is."

"First you must promise not to say anything."

Werner narrows his eyes. "First you must show me."

Helmuth won't show him, not without a promise. He sticks his hands into his pockets, walks away, whistling. He can feel Werner's curiosity. That's good. Let his curiosity simmer.

A few days later, Helmuth tries again. This time he brings Düwer along as he shows Werner a brochure.

Werner grows white around his mouth as he reads over the pamphlet. "No way," he says, shoving the pamphlet back at Helmuth. "I'm too busy for this."

Helmuth eyes Werner closely. Werner looks angry. Has Helmuth made a terrible mistake? His hands shake as he folds the leaflet, slips it into his pocket. At that moment, their boss, Heinrich Mohns, passes the doorway, pokes his head in. "What's going on here?"

Düwer elbows Werner, a warning to keep quiet.

Helmuth pretends to be unruffled. "I hoped Werner could help me with a little homework, with something I didn't understand," he tells his boss.

Herr Mohns stares at Helmuth and then Werner. "Get to work," he says at last. "We don't pay you for socializing."

Helmuth and Düwer return to their desks. Helmuth feels Mohns's eyes on him, wishes he would stop staring. Helmuth buries himself in his work but he can't concentrate, not with Herr Mohns's eyes boring into his back.

February 5. Two-thirty. The office grows suddenly quiet as two Gestapo agents stride purposefully through the office door.

"Helmuth Hübener?" says the taller agent to Helmuth.

Helmuth's mouth turns dry. He licks his lips, nods, and says, "Yes."

"You know why we are here," says the agent.

It isn't a question. It's a statement.

Helmuth glances at Werner, who doesn't look up, only stares at a green file folder on his desk. Herr Mohns stands in the doorway, looking gleeful. Helmuth understands the look. Herr Mohns is a man who has done his duty.

"Come with us," says the agent. He nods to Düwer. "You, too."

Helmuth goes for his coat, but the agents yank him back, push him toward the door. He falters, recovers his step. Outside, the boys slide into the backseat of a black Mercedes, are swallowed up inside, flanked by the two Gestapo officers.

∞

With each tick of the pocket watch, Helmuth's heart pounds harder. Herr Ranke glances down at an official-looking paper. He begins to read slowly and clearly, enunciating each word importantly:

"'On the eleventh of August 1942 the court found Helmuth Hübener guilty of listening to a foreign radio station and distributing the news heard in connection with conspiracy to commit high treason and treasonable support of the enemy.'"

Must not breathe, must keep hope swallowed inside, must not let hope fly out of throat.

"'He is sentenced to death and the loss of civil rights during his lifetime.'"

The words begin to shoot around the cell, exploding off the walls, striking Helmuth like bullets.

Bang. *The National Minister of Justice has decreed that there will be no clemency.*

Bang. *Justice will run its course.*

Bang. *The execution of the judgment will take place on 27 October 1942 after eight* P.M.

Tonight.

The floor buckles beneath Helmuth and the walls waver. The single lightbulb overhead throbs, hurts his eyes, burns into his skull. He closes his eyes, squeezes them shut, won't let the tears escape, wills them away.

Helmuth opens his eyes. The men are still there. The prison guards grip their truncheons, pulsing pulsing pulsing.

"Have you any final requests?" asks Herr Ranke.

Helmuth licks his dry lips. "Yes," he whispers hoarsely. "I would like to write letters to my family."

"So be it," says Herr Ranke.

Their job done, the men turn on their heels and, one by one, leave the cell. Single file. Slam. Click. *The cell door bolts shut.*

Helmuth reaches for the wall behind him, sinks to the floor, clutches his belly, lets out a deep wail. Hope flies from his chest, flutters around the room, beats against the window.

∞

Four-thirty P.M. Helmuth stands in the police interrogation room, waiting. He takes in the padded black leather door. Gleaming wooden desk. Green blotter. File folders. Straight-backed wooden chairs. The slightly burned smell of real coffee. Two white china cups. Two saucers. Two silver teaspoons. It all looks so normal. Civilized. Like a banker's office.

He wonders if they will beat him, wonders if he can hold up. Remembers his promise to Karl and Rudi. *No names.* Remembers Brother Worbs. *You'll admit to anything to stop the pain.* Shakes the thought from his head. He will take one step at a time. He will find out what they know. Admit nothing.

Helmuth hears the stamp of feet in the hall, two crisp "*Heil* Hitler"s. The door swings open. The same two agents enter — Wangemann and Müssner, Helmuth has learned — and barely acknowledge him.

The taller man, Müssner, sets his briefcase on the table with a thump. Unbuckles it. Shuffles several papers into a neat pile on the desk.

Helmuth's stomach tightens. Fliers. His fliers.

"Sit," says Wangemann. He's shorter, more squarely built.

Helmuth sits. Wangemann stands next to Helmuth, arms folded.

Müssner picks up the first leaflet, waves it carelessly as if it were a simple grocery list. "This was found in a telephone booth in the Luisenweg-Süderstrasse at nine o'clock in the morning." He fans out the others. "The rest were found in stairwells and mailboxes at Süderstrasse 205. All brought in by good citizens."

Wangemann leans in. His breath smells of onions. "Do you know why you've been arrested?"

Helmuth looks at him blankly. Hopes.

"You're accused of distributing enemy propaganda. Do you have any idea what this means for you, distributing enemy propaganda?"

Helmuth corrects him. "Allegedly —"

Wangemann's fist smashes into Helmuth's face. Knocks him to the floor. A black boot kicks him in the stomach, twice. Helmuth curls, knees to his chest, arms shielding his head, gasping for air.

"You want the government to fall, but who's fallen now?" shrieks Wangemann. He kicks Helmuth in the ribs. Again. And again. "Get up," he says. "Now let's see how you stand."

Helmuth wobbles. He reaches for the chair. It hurts to stand straight. He tries to take a deep breath. His ribs burn.

"You might as well confess," says Müssner. "Things will go better for you, the way they're going better for your friend Gerhard Düwer. He's told us everything."

That shocks Helmuth. Not Düwer. It can't be. It's a trap, he tells himself.

"You don't believe us?" says Müssner. "You think it's a trap?"

Müssner flips open a file, selects a typed sheet, reads from it: "'One day, it could have been the middle of January, Hübener handed me a typewritten paper and asked me to read it. I read the paper and without saying anything, I hid it and took it home. I could tell at once it was inflammatory writing against Germany.'"

Helmuth's ears fill up, as though he's underwater.

Müssner looks at Helmuth, and when he speaks, his words sound underwater, too. "Your friend is a good German who only wants to do his duty." He continues to read from Düwer's statement. "'At home, I locked the paper in a box because I wanted to gather evidence, so that at the right time, I could denounce Hübener.'"

The word rings in Helmuth's ears. *Denounce denounce denounce.*

Müssner continues reading. "'I realize that I was wrong, and I now fall under suspicion for having cooperated with Hübener. This is not the case, however, and I want to clarify that I merely wanted to collect evidence against Hübener.'"

Müssner stops, clasps his hands together, rests them on the desk. "Have you anything to say?"

Helmuth's heart sinks as he realizes that Düwer denounced him in order to save himself. *You'll admit to anything to stop the pain.* That's what Brother Worbs had said. What did the Gestapo do to Düwer?

Helmuth sees Karl's grinning face, Rudi's worried face. He feels their hands, three hands, one atop the other, shaking on their promise. *Agreed. No names.*

"I'm ready to confess," says Helmuth. "I take full responsibility."

Later, the black Mercedes carrying Helmuth threads through the Hammerbrook streets. Helmuth prays Oma isn't home, so that she won't see his bruised face, but she is home, and she cries out and rushes to him, reaching for him. "Helmuth, what have you done?"

Wangemann thrusts out his hand, stops her, says, "Official Gestapo business. We're looking for enemy propaganda."

"Enemy propaganda!" says Oma. "We don't have any —"

Opa guides Oma to the sofa, saying, "Quiet, dear, let them look. They'll see that they're mistaken, that all this is a terrible mistake."

Oma clutches her apron. Wrings it. Weeps loudly. Opa draws her to him, a stricken look on his face, and Helmuth can't watch anymore. He points to the closet, his bedroom, says everything can be found there.

But the two agents ransack the apartment anyway. Oma whimpers as they empty drawers, lift mattresses, peeling wallpaper for secret hideaways. In the end, they find all the incriminating evidence just where Helmuth said — the Rola radio, a pile of assorted leaflets, notebooks, manuscripts of handbills, shorthand notes, and the Remington typewriter with seven carbon sheets of paper stuck between the carriage rollers.

"Such interesting reading," says Müssner sarcastically, leaning over the typewriter. "It says, 'Who is inciting whom?'" He reads a section out loud. "'All accusations against the American government . . . lack any truthful basis. They are fabricated, malicious, and remain symptoms of the deepest hatred — '"

Wangemann glares, apelike, at Helmuth. "So you think the Führer is a liar."

Helmuth wants to shout out, "Yes! He is a liar!" But instead he clamps his mouth shut, steels himself, prays Wangemann won't hit him, not here, not in front of his grandmother.

"You disgusting piece of trash," says Wangemann. He pushes Helmuth out the door, out to the street. Oma wails behind him, and as he ducks into the car he looks up, sees her glistening face at the window.

Eight P.M. A green prisoner van transports Helmuth to Concentration Camp Fuhlsbüttel to the north of Hamburg. A guard takes his trousers, his shirt, his shoelaces, and hands him a pair of blue prison pants and shirt. Leads him to a holding cell.

Helmuth looks around the putrid cell. An overflowing slop bucket in the corner. A cot with no mattress, just boards. A single lightbulb hanging from the ceiling. Somewhere he hears a scream, sobs.

He sits on the bed, swings his legs over the edge of the cot, lies down. He folds his arms across his chest for warmth. Closes his eyes. Tells himself the worst is over. He's confessed. He kept his promise to Rudi and Karl.

Tears swell and then come in great heaves of relief.

∞

Helmuth sits on the floor beneath the window in a square of sunlight. He can barely breathe when he thinks what lies ahead. He focuses his mind, doesn't want to be numb. Wants to think, to feel. He listens to the sounds of prison. From the hall, a metallic clattering sound, doors opening, doors closing. From another cell, sobs. From a passing guard, footfalls. From the prison yard, the tramp of feet. From the city, sirens.

The square of sunshine moves, diffuses, grows faint yellow. Helmuth feels lost in a dream. Karl and Rudi enter the dream. Their faces float in front of him, then fade out, and enter again, first one, then the other, and then the three of them together.

∞

Morning. The slot opens. A cup of brown liquid and a hunk of dry bread. Helmuth gulps the liquid, gobbles the bread. He can no longer avoid the overflowing slop bucket.

Later. Footsteps. Outside the cell door. Helmuth stands in anticipation. The slot slides open. Eyes meet his. The slot slams shut. A key turns in the lock, a rasping, grating sound, metal against metal. The door swings open.

A guard looms in the open door. "Out," he says, motioning with the rubber truncheon. "Back to police headquarters with you."

Helmuth falters. "But I've already confessed."

The guard's mouth tightens. *Wham.* His truncheon strikes Helmuth in the stomach, so fast he doesn't see it coming. It doubles him over. Knocks the wind out of him. Helmuth groans, clutches his belly. The sour taste of vomit. He swallows it down.

"Guess you didn't tell them enough," says the guard. "Hands on head!"

It stabs to stand up straight. Helmuth clasps his hands on top of his head, walks, elbows sticking out like wings. He plods down the corridor, outside to the transport van.

Gestapo headquarters. Helmuth awaits his turn for interrogation in a room painted a brilliant, dazzling white and brightly lit with large lights. It's called the "Hall of Mirrors," a Nazi joke, Helmuth supposes, because there are no mirrors. All around, blue-clad prisoners stand at attention, noses one inch from the white wall, never moving, never flinching.

One hour. Two. More. Helmuth's legs ache. His stomach burns. He feels faint. His mouth is dry. Needs the toilet, worries he cannot hold it, doesn't want to think about the trouble that will cause.

His name is called. The Gestapo interrogation room has a concrete floor. Round metal drains. A hose looped in the corner. Dark splatters — dried blood? — across whitewashed walls. A lingering scent of disinfectant. In the center, a wooden table. Two wooden chairs.

"We know you didn't work alone," says Wangemann, tapping his truncheon against his palm.

"But I did," says Helmuth.

This time Helmuth expects the blows, the kicks, the grind of boots.

The transport van carries him back to Fuhlsbüttel, where the guard clamps his hands and feet in metal bands, cuffs the bands to the bed. "For stubborn ones," says the guard. "You're a tough one. Most crack within twenty-four hours. Maybe you'll give a better answer tomorrow."

Helmuth lies spread-eagled on the boards. His face back shoulders buttocks legs they burn burn burn. He prays, not for deliverance, but for strength. He will not crack. Must. Hold. Out. No. Names.

Another interrogation. Helmuth gasps for breath. Each breath burns. His whole body feels on fire, and he cannot hold out any longer, cannot stop himself as he croaks, "Karl-Heinz Schnibbe. Rudi Wobbe."

Helmuth sits on the edge of the cot, head in hands, and sobs. Huge, wracking sobs. He hates himself, hates what he has done.

If only he held out.

If only they had killed him.

Helmuth wishes he could kill himself. But how! He has no shoelaces. No sheet. He lies on the cot, stares at the ceiling. Holds his breath, gasps, and gives up. Clutches his throat. Squeezes. Hard. Gasps again. Tries again. Harder. No use.

And then he realizes: He can't die, he mustn't die, he must live.

Live, to take the blame.

Live, to save Karl and Rudi.

The SS sit at a large table in the middle of the room. Talking, laughing, shuffling papers. Helmuth tunes out the guards, narrows his eyes to slits, blocks out the dazzling wall, stands, nose one inch from the wall. Nothing fazes him. Nothing detracts him. He knows what he must do.

The Gestapo are precise. Methodical.

The Gestapo don't make mistakes.

Neither will Helmuth.

He has learned to do the waiting right, not to concentrate too hard, not to faint, not to attract attention, knows the terrible blows and kicks that fainting brings. Knows not to drink in the morning, no matter how thirsty, because at the Hall of Mirrors, prisoners aren't allowed to use the toilet. And when it's his turn for interrogation, he will stick to his story, take all the blame for the radio and the leaflets, convince the Gestapo that Karl and Rudi were just curious onlookers, that Karl and Rudi are not traitors, that the leaflet campaign was all his idea.

The Gestapo are precise, methodical.

The Gestapo don't make mistakes.

Neither will Helmuth. He will do it right. If only he could warn Karl and Rudi. He squeezes his eyes shut. Prays.

Suddenly the door opens and another prisoner is brought into the Hall of Mirrors. Out of the corner of his swollen eye, Helmuth sees Karl.

The Gestapo have made a mistake!

Helmuth nearly makes a mistake, too. He nearly calls out to Karl. It takes all his strength to swallow the words in his throat. His throat tightens, swollen thick with words.

Karl spots him, too, and a stricken look crosses his

face. *Keepwalkingkeepwalkingkeepwalking,* wills Helmuth, and Karl does. Ten steps. Six steps. Three steps from Helmuth, and at that moment, that precise moment, their eyes lock. Helmuth twitches the left side of his mouth, the slightest smile, winks his left eye, not enough to attract guard's attention, just enough to signal Karl.

Karl blinks, hesitates, and then a flicker of understanding passes over his face. Helmuth swallows hard, gulps down a sob. He's sure that Karl understands, sure that Karl knows that Helmuth has taken the blame, sure Karl understands not to say anything that will implicate himself more during his interrogation.

Helmuth blinks back tears. Wishes he could warn Rudi, wishes he could save them both from interrogation, wishes he could tell them he tried to hold out, wishes he could ask for their forgiveness.

But there is no way to warn Rudi, and Helmuth does not see him or Karl or Düwer again until the trial six months later at the People's Court in Berlin.

The infamous Blood Tribunal.

The highest, most feared court in Germany.

∞

Six P.M. *A prison guard brings Helmuth paper, a fountain pen, blue ink. For his final letters. The paper, the pen, the ink — - they are sweeter than Mutti's plum* Kuchen.

Helmuth pulls up his stool to the scratchy table, spreads out the first sheet of paper, smooths it with his hands. He knuckles away tears. What will he tell his family? That he was foolish to think he could wage battle against such evil?

No. Helmuth does not believe he was foolish. He did not risk his life in vain. God can bring good out of evil, but God can't do it alone. God needs people. People who will stand up. People who will dare to speak out. For what has a man profited, if he has gained the whole world and lost his soul? That's what the Bible says.

Helmuth feels something. His chest swells. A warm calmness fills him, and he knows that he has lived a life that stood for something.

∞

August 4, 1942. Helmuth leaves for Berlin. A guard handcuffs him, leads him to a green prisoner transport van.

Helmuth climbs inside, and his heart leaps as he sees Karl and Rudi sitting there. Gerhard Düwer, too. Each boy is handcuffed to a guard, and so all Helmuth can do is smile, and smile he does. They all grin at one another, all except for Düwer, who casts his eyes down, and stares at his hands folded in his lap. He cannot look Helmuth in the eye.

But Helmuth waits for Düwer to look at him, wills

Düwer to look at him, and when he does, Helmuth nods and smiles. A mixture of shame and relief crosses Düwer's face. *I'm sorry,* he mouths, his eyes pained. *Me, too,* says Helmuth with a nod. *Me, too.*

The boys ride in silence. At the Altona train station, the guards herd them into a special train compartment marked: PRISONER TRANSPORT — ENTRY *VERBOTEN*.

Once inside, the guards uncuff the boys. Rudi's guard says, "If I were the judge, I would give you boys a good thrashing, put you in uniform, and ship you to the front. Let the punishment fit the crime, that's what I say."

Karl's guard nods, agrees, then points the boys to a bench seat. "Sit. You may talk, but I'm warning you, do not stand up and not one word about your case."

The guards sit across from the four boys, take out a deck of playing cards. Helmuth looks at Rudi and Karl. Hot tears flood his eyes. "I'm sorry," he whispers to them. "I tried to hold out."

His guard shoots a warning look. "Not one word about your case!" he says firmly.

Helmuth falls quiet. Karl cups his hand over Helmuth's, squeezes. So does Rudi. The three friends sit there for the longest while, one hand atop the other.

It is Karl who breaks the silence first. "Remember when I brought the false teeth to church?" he says. Helmuth remembers, and he laughs. For the rest of the trip, the boys swap stories.

Moabit Prison, Berlin. Helmuth meets his court-appointed lawyer, Herr Doctor Knie. He's a nervous man wearing a crooked red bow tie and a Nazi party pin on his lapel. He spends the short time rifling through papers, asking simple questions, but not taking any notes. Helmuth's heart sinks. His lawyer does not work for him. He works for the Nazi government.

Nighttime. Another sleepless night. Helmuth goes over the terrible interrogations again and again, turning each over in his head. Wants to be able to recall each detail so that he's consistent in his answers.

August 11, 1942. The People's Court. The four boys are hustled into the courtroom. Helmuth wears the same clothes he wore the day of his arrest, seven months ago. His trousers hang loosely, his white collared shirt flutters about, so thin he has grown. It is the same with his friends. But they have been permitted to shower with real soap, and so they look scrubbed.

The courtroom has dark oak floors. Dark wood-paneled walls. Three bloodred-swastika black banners hang from ceiling to floor. A large portrait of Adolf Hitler. And it's packed with spectators, mostly reporters. Murmurs ripple over the room as the boys enter.

A guard uncuffs Karl, Rudi, and Gerhard, but Helmuth is left cuffed, his hands chained behind his back. That tells Helmuth something. That the justices have already decided he is the most important criminal, that he has committed a most serious offense. He feels nauseous. The more serious the justices consider the offense, the less likely that Helmuth will be tried as a juvenile.

Helmuth looks around the crowded room, spots Herr Doctor Knie. Gestapo agent Müssner. Heinrich Mohns, his boss from the Bieberhaus, wearing his Nazi Party uniform. Werner Kranz, the apprentice. Werner looks pained, as if dragged there by the scruff of his neck. Herr Schnibbe, Karl's father. No Mutti. No Oma or Opa. Helmuth is relieved. He couldn't bear to see their anguished faces.

At ten o'clock the tall wooden doors swing open, and the courtroom falls quiet. At once, everyone rises as seven justices enter. Three wear bloodred caps and flowing red robes with a large golden eagle emblazoned on the front. The others wear stiffly pressed SS and military uniforms. There is no jury. The justices are the jury.

The trial opens with a slam of the gavel that rings throughout the courtroom. One of the red-robed justices — Justice Engert — asks the boys simple questions — name, birth date, residence, occupation — and then reviews the charges against each boy. *Deliberate listening to foreign radio stations . . . Willfully distributing newscasts of foreign radio stations . . . Conspiracy to commit high treason.*

Chief Justice Fikeis takes over, barking out question after question, testing each boy's knowledge about Adolf Hitler and the Nazi Party. "Wobbe, what is our Führer's birthday?" "Schnibbe, what are the words to the 'Horst Wessel'?" "Düwer, how many points in the Nazi Program?" Helmuth gets the hardest questions. "Hübener, what are the political aims for the Nazi Party?" He answers each question sharply.

Witnesses are called. Werner Kranz and Heinrich Mohns recount the events of January 20, when Herr Mohns caught Helmuth trying to press a leaflet into Werner's hand.

Gestapo agent Müssner details each interrogation, word by word from his notes, saying things like, "after lengthy remonstrations" and "after emphatic admonishments Hübener was moved to make a confession about the extent of his destructive activity."

Helmuth grunts at the words. That's what the Gestapo call beatings and torture. Remonstrations and admonishments.

The justices don't miss a detail from the boys' lives: their Party record books, their school records, their Hitler Youth records, even Rudi's Lord Lister Detective card becomes evidence against them.

Soon the questioning turns to the boys' crime. Justice Fikeis rehashes the same questions the boys had answered under interrogation, but there's a different edge to his questions now. Helmuth concentrates, tries to put his finger on the shift.

Slowly it dawns on Helmuth: Fikeis is questioning them as adults. They are all being tried as adults, not juveniles.

Hot fear spreads through Helmuth. An adult conviction means much worse. A longer prison sentence or possibly the death sentence. He can't let that happen.

Helmuth focuses, clears his mind. He knows what he must do: He must keep the attention of the justices, he must convince them that he was the ringleader, that Karl and Rudi and Düwer were simply followers, no matter what.

It's Helmuth's turn. Chief Justice Fikeis takes out the pamphlets and fliers and clears the courtroom to protect the spectators from the enemy propaganda. The sight of the pamphlets and fliers enrages the judge. "Why did you write these?" he barks at Helmuth.

"To let the people know the truth," answers Helmuth in a loud, clear voice. The other justices fall deathly silent. He can feel Karl, Rudi, and Düwer stiffen next to him. But Helmuth knows what he's doing. There's no other way.

"Do you really believe that the British are telling the truth?" says Fikeis.

"Absolutely. Don't you?"

Fikeis's face grows purple with rage. "Do you doubt Germany's ultimate victory?"

"Do you actually believe that Germany *can* win the war?"

Justice Fikeis is screaming now: "Are you suggesting that your leaders are lying?"

Helmuth takes a deep breath, and in the most contemptible manner he can muster, says, *"Jawohl, ihr lügt."* Yes, you are all liars!

Pandemonium breaks out among the justices. Helmuth's attorney snaps back, scowls at Helmuth as if to say, *Are you crazy?*

Helmuth's insolence launches Justice Fikeis to his feet. He leans over the bench, purple with rage. "You snot-nosed kid, what do you know about war? You are scum! A traitor!" He snaps the file shut, addresses Helmuth's attorney: "Is there anything else you'd like to say?"

Herr Doctor Knie argues that Helmuth succumbed to the enemy propaganda because he was too immature to resist the temptation. "I ask the court to be lenient, in consideration of his age," says the attorney.

"That's enough!" Fikeis glares at Helmuth. "Hübener is no average boy." He brings another paper out of a folder. Helmuth recognizes the paper: It's his graduation essay, "The War of the Plutocrats."

Fikeis rattles the essay at Helmuth's attorney. "This is the work of a person far above eighteen years. This is no immature youth! The people must be protected from traitors like him! The Fatherland is at stake!"

He replaces the essay, claps the folder shut, slams his fist down on top. "This defendant acted with the thought and cunning of an adult! Consequently he is to be sentenced as an adult. Without exception this precocious young man has long since outgrown his youth."

Justice Fikeis beckons to the two other justices.

They hover behind the bench before drawing back to their chairs. "We are ready for sentencing," says Fikeis.

The courtroom doors swing open, and the spectators fill their seats. Helmuth's heart pounds against his rib cage as Justice Fikeis begins. "The court orders the following to be sentenced," he says in a smug, satisfied voice. "Hübener, for listening to a foreign radio station and distributing the news heard in connection with conspiracy to commit high treason and treasonable support of the enemy: *to death and the loss of his civil rights during his lifetime.*"

All around Helmuth, the courtroom, the justices, the swastika banners explode. Red white yellow blue streak his eyes. His knees buckle. The guard yanks him to his feet. He hears Fikeis pronounce, "Wobbe . . . conspiracy to commit high treason . . . *ten years imprisonment.* Schnibbe . . . *five years imprisonment.* Düwer . . . *four years imprisonment.* . . . The defendants are to bear the costs of the proceedings."

"Have you anything to say?" said Fikeis. "Düwer?"

"No."

"Schnibbe?"

"No."

"Wobbe?"

"No."

"Hübener?"

Helmuth struggles to regain his thoughts, to bring the pieces together. He points a finger at the justices. "All I did was tell the truth, and you have sentenced me to die, just for telling the truth. My time is now but your time will come!"

The courtroom erupts in a roar.

"Shut up!" screams Justice Fikeis. "Push him down! Shut him up!" His gavel slams again and again.

The guards leap upon Helmuth, force him to his seat. His heart slams against his rib cage. He gulps for air. He did the right thing. He knows he did. Otherwise, the justices would execute them all.

The trial is over. The boys are shackled and led to a small holding cell in the basement. A guard removes the handcuffs from Karl, Rudi, and Düwer, but leaves Helmuth shackled.

"Helmuth!" cries Rudi. "Why did you do that?"

"Because it's the truth," says Helmuth. He feels his eyes well with tears and he blinks them away. "I did the right thing. I have no regrets."

"They will reduce or cancel the verdict," says Karl. "You're too young."

"No," says Helmuth. "They will make an example out of me."

A guard returns, says, "Wobbe, Schnibbe, Düwer, get ready to go. You're going back to Hamburg."

The boys surround Helmuth, embrace him tightly. "We'll meet again," says Karl.

"Good-bye, my friends," says Helmuth. "We *will* meet again."

∞

Helmuth huffs the ink dry on the last letter. It is 8:05 P.M. He reads it again, wonders what his family will think, wonders who will tell Mutti. He feels sad for Mutti. He knows his death will be hard on her. For Oma and Opa, too. And Hans and Gerhard. He hopes his letters comfort them. Bring them solace.

The brusque pound of feet. The jangle of keys. The scrape of metal against metal. Helmuth stands, ready. He has made up his mind to go quietly, with dignity and courage.

The door swings open. Two guards enter. "Prisoner Hübener, come with us," says one. "It is time." The other shackles Helmuth's hands behind his back.

Helmuth walks without stumbling, down the long corridor, outside into the courtyard. He draws in the crisp night air. It feels good. It smells like Mutti's sheets on wash day.

Above the tall redbrick execution shed, between the leafless

tree branches, the moon is full, opalescent, and he remembers a
night long ago:

　　Mutti tucking them in,

　　three brothers,

　　three dark heads nestled against white pillows,

　　white moonlight shimmering the walls,

　　and Helmuth is floating.

∞

Twenty-foot wall surrounding Plötzensee prison in Berlin, Germany. (Photo taken by the author)

AUTHOR'S NOTE

March 17, 2004. It's morning. Soft gray light slips over the tall redbrick wall that surrounds Plötzensee. It stretches across the exercise yard and reaches through the arched windows of the execution chamber. Inside, the light slants across the concrete floor. A vase of flowers and a single evergreen wreath sit where the guillotine once stood.

I am standing where Helmuth stood during the last eighteen seconds of his life. I am standing where nearly 2,200 other men and women stood before they faced the executioner at Plötzensee between the years 1940 and 1945. Many of these victims were sentenced to death as "enemies of the state" because they — like Helmuth Hübener — fought for human rights, political freedom, and truth.

This story is a work of historical fiction: Helmuth Hübener was a real person and his character is based on extensive research — all filtered through my imagination in order to create a dramatic meditation on what Helmuth, his family, and friends lived through.

In a work of fiction in which characters and events are based on real people and their experiences, it is natural for readers to wonder: What really happened?

We don't know exactly how Helmuth spent his last day on earth. To create scenes, I extracted factual details from his prison records and other primary sources. For other details, I relied on the experiences and writings of people who lived through similar experiences.

We also don't know exactly what Helmuth wrote in his last letters. No copies remain. But Helmuth's half brother, Gerhard Kunkel, remembers his own letter from Helmuth.

"I was in Russia when I got Helmuth's letter," Gerhard told me. "I burned it, worried that it could get me into trouble. But I memorized the words. It said, *I am very grateful to my Father in Heaven that this agonizing life will shortly come to end this evening. I could not stand it any longer. My Father in Heaven knows that I have done nothing wrong. I know that God lives and that He will be the judge in this matter. Until our happy reunion in a better world, I remain your brother in the Gospel. Helmuth.*"

Helmuth's arrest shocked Gerhard, who received the news at officer training school in Warsaw, Poland. "It was like a ton of bricks hit me," said Gerhard. "Here I was in the German army, and he's doing things like that against the government. It hit me hard."

Gerhard was court-martialed. "For three days I was squeezed [interrogated]," said Gerhard. "I never knew at any moment if they were going to take me out and shoot me as a traitor."

The Nazis punished Gerhard for delivering the radio, condemning him as *"Statspolitisch nicht zuferlässig,"* or politically unreliable. "They took my rank away," said Gerhard. "I was a Lieutenant, and they demoted me to Corporal."

Gerhard was sent to the Russian front as a forward artillery observer. He fought in Russia, and later in Italy. Wounded three times, he received the Iron Cross, the Medal of Valor, and the Russian Battle Medal. For his actions, he earned back his rank and was released from the rehabilitation unit.

The day after Helmuth was executed, his mother, Emma Guddat Kunkel Hübener, read about her son's death in the newspaper. She later received an invoice of expenses for Helmuth's execution: 1.50 Reichsmarks for each day Helmuth was imprisoned, 300 Reichsmarks for the cost of his execution, and 12 Pfennig for the cost of mailing the invoice. In late July 1943, Emma and her parents died in massive bombing attacks on Hamburg that killed an estimated 43,000 people.

Shocked by Helmuth's harsh sentence, many people wrote letters on his behalf, including his stepfather, Hugo Hübener. After the war, Hugo visited Gerhard several times. "I was surprised by how much he had changed," said Gerhard. "He brought us some wood so that we could have some fire in the stove and make some food. And he even came to church with us. He sat through all the sessions and listened to all the singing and the music. He was a different Hugo. It tells me that people can change, if they want to change."

Another letter was written by one of the interrogating Gestapo agents — either Müssner or Wangemann. The signature is illegible, but the letter writer describes Helmuth as "mentally uncorrupted" and "intelligent but not mature enough to recognize the consequences of his actions." The agent argues that Helmuth's graduation paper proves that he had "a positive attitude toward the state and the Führer."

The Senior District Director of the Hamburg Hitler Youth also wrote on Helmuth's behalf, saying that Helmuth "served to the fullest satisfaction of his superiors."

Another Hitler Youth official from the Berlin headquarters, however, claimed that Helmuth's Hitler Youth record didn't matter. In a letter, this official argued for the execution, due to "the severity of Hübener's crime" and the dangerous effect it could have on German morale during the war.

Karl-Heinz Schnibbe was sentenced to five years in a concentration camp, whereas Rudi Wobbe received a harsher sentence. For the lighter sentence, Karl credits Helmuth's warning to him in the Hall of Mirrors. "He gave me a kind of wink and grin," said Karl. "I caught it out of the corner of my eye as I went in. At that moment, I knew that he had kept his promise."

On their way to the trial in Berlin, Helmuth apologized to Karl and Rudi for giving up their names to the Gestapo. "I'm sorry," Helmuth told them. "I couldn't stand it [the torture] any longer." Helmuth also forgave Gerhard Düwer for denouncing him, saying, "I'm not mad at you. I know you could not help it."

At the trial, Karl noted that the judges focused on Helmuth and the leaflets, firing question after question at him. It was clear that the People's Court intended to make an example out of him. "Helmuth realized he was doomed," said Karl.

To Karl, that explains why Helmuth purposely angered the justices with his responses: to save the lives of his friends. "To this day, I'm amazed at how cool, how clear, and how smart Helmuth was," said Karl. "I believe he had made up his mind to conduct himself with courage and dignity."

Toward the end of the war, as Germany needed more manpower, the Nazis offered Karl the opportunity to restore his honor by fighting for Germany. In return, he would be released from prison. Karl accepted, and he was sent to Czechoslovakia, where he was captured by the Russians and shipped to a prisoner-of-war camp in Siberia. The Russians released Karl in 1949, four years after the war ended.

Karl emigrated to the United States in 1952.

Helmuth couldn't warn Rudi Wobbe, who implicated himself more during his interrogation and to a prison cellmate who betrayed him to the Gestapo. Rudi was given a ten-year sentence, but he was released after Germany surrendered in 1945. He emigrated to the United States in 1953.

Gerhard Düwer received a four-year sentence in return for his cooperation with authorities. Unlike Karl-Heinz Schnibbe, Düwer could not be inducted into the German army because he had trouble with his feet and limped badly. At the end of the war, Düwer was released from prison.

After the war, Karl befriended Gerhard Düwer. "He told me he was ashamed about the way he denounced

Helmuth," said Karl. "He apologized and I forgave — just as Helmuth had done. There's no reason to hold a grudge or to hate. If you forgive, you're forgiven."

Karl explained his capacity for forgiveness. "Who's perfect?" said Karl. "Not you or I. People cannot judge. They have no idea how it really was, how the Gestapo will get information out of you."

Fellow church member Heinrich Worbs died shortly after his release from the concentration camp.

It is unknown what became of Helmuth's fellow apprentice Werner Kranz, whom Helmuth had approached to translate the leaflets into French.

On May 12, 1950, Heinrich Mohns, the political overseer who reported Helmuth to the Gestapo, was tried and convicted as a war criminal. He received a two-year prison sentence for "crimes against humanity," but his sentence was later nullified.

Helmuth's Oberbau teacher, August Meins, described Helmuth as a modest, diligent, likeable student. But it was obvious to Meins that Helmuth did not agree with the principles of National Socialism. "I could always observe his reaction, his eyes, when different things were discussed by the class. Many times, I could tell he thought like me," said Meins. "But we never spoke about his thoughts or our thoughts. It was too dangerous."

Still, when Meins learned about Helmuth's anti-Nazi activities and his subsequent arrest, he was plagued by one question. "How did he come to the resistance? Wasn't it stupidity? He had to know that resistance was pointless."

The teacher's question is one that Helmuth's own brother Gerhard Kunkel has asked himself. "I was angry at the Nazis. They could have handled Helmuth a little different. He was no adult — he was still a teenager," Gerhard told me. "But I was also angry at Helmuth. He should have known better than that, being as smart as he was. He knew the laws of the land. A sixteen-year-old boy cannot change the government."

Gerhard and his brother Hans emigrated to the United States in 1952.

There are many reasons for a person to lie, but to have a reason to tell the truth, you must have a deep belief. And great courage. Helmuth possessed these things — and held on to them even when the Nazis called him a traitor and sentenced him to death.

Helmuth Hübener is a boy who dared to speak out for the truth.

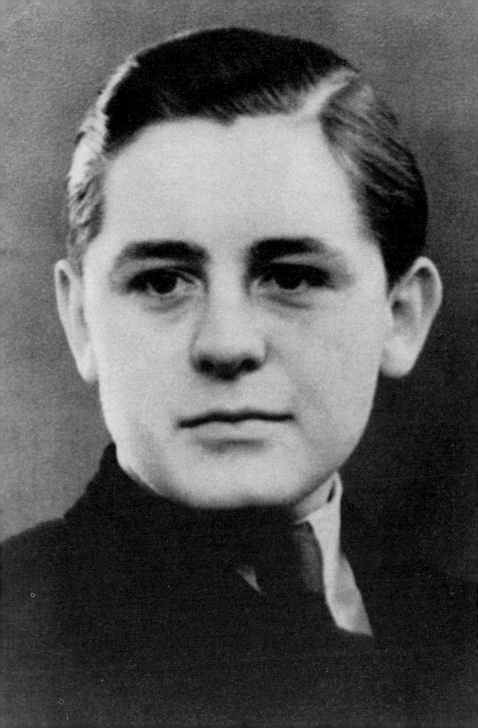

Helmuth and his family. (Left to right) Oma (Wilhelmina Sudrow), Helmuth (about 2), Opa (Johannes Sudrow), Gerhard (about 6), Hans (about 7), and Mutti (Emma). (Photograph circa 1927. Courtesy Gerhard Kunkel)

Helmut Guddat Hübener, shortly before his arrest, age 16. (Courtesy Karl-Heinz Schnibbe)

Gerhard Gustav Kunkel, age 18. (Courtesy Gerhard Kunkel)

Rudi Wobbe, Helmuth Guddat Hübener, and Karl-Heinz Schnibbe. (Photograph circa 1941. Courtesy Karl-Heinz Schnibbe)

Helmuth Guddat Hübener. (Photo circa 1940. Courtesy Karl-Heinz Schnibbe)

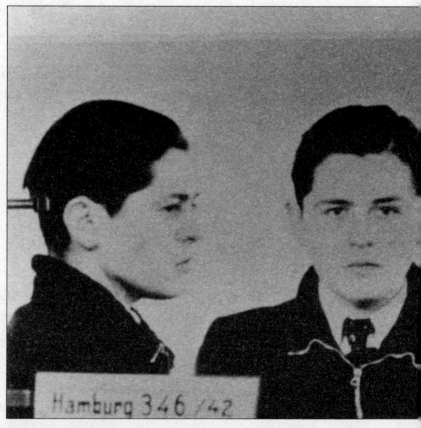

Gestapo photographs of Helmuth Guddat Hübener, taken February 1942.
(Courtesy Karl-Heinz Schnibbe)

Red poster announcing Helmuth's execution. (Courtesy Karl-Heinz Schnibbe)

ung.

f wegen Vorbereitung
zünftigung zum Tode
hrenrechte verurteilte

-ner

Volksgerichtshof.

TRANSLATION:

Let It Be Known.

On 11 August, 1942, the People's Court sentenced 17-year-old Helmuth Hübener of Hamburg, to being stripped of his citizen's rights, and in addition, to death, because of his treasonous support of the enemy. His execution has been carried out today, the 27th of October, by the order of the chief attorney gereral of the People's Court.

Karl-Heinz Schnibbe (left); Helmuth (center); Rudi Wobbe. Photo taken at memorial service in Helmuth's honor in Hamburg, Germany in 1985.
(Photo courtesy Karl-Heinz Schnibbe)

Gerhard Kunkel, August 2005. (Photo taken by the author)

Memorial wreath for Helmuth in his execution chamber,
Plötzensee prison, Berlin, Germany, 2004.
(Photo taken by the author)

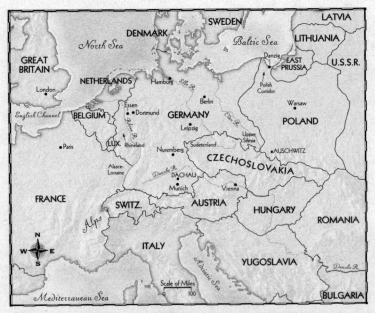

This map illustrates the borders of Europe in 1936, as established by the Treaty of Versailles at the end of the first World War. That year, Adolf Hitler violated the treaty when he remilitarized the Rhineland.

In 1938, he annexed Austria and Sudetenland, and in early 1939, Czechoslovakia. Each time he violated the treaty, he continued to promise world leaders and the German people that he wanted peace, not war. In September 1939, he invaded Poland.

THIRD REICH TIME LINE

1918

- The Great War, later known as the First World War, ends (November).

1919

- The Treaty of Versailles is signed (June).
- The German Reich, known today as the Weimar Republic, is established as the official government in Germany (August). Today, most historians agree that the harsh Treaty of Versailles helped create the conditions responsible for Hitler's rise to power.

1923

- Adolf Hitler and his Storm Troopers are arrested, for attempting to overthrow the Reich (November).

1924

- Hitler is found guilty of treason. From his jail cell, he pens a propagandistic and political autobiography, *Mein Kampf.* Hitler released from jail (December).

1925

- Adolf Hitler begins to rebuild the Nazi Party (March).

1926

- Hitlerjugend (Hitler Youth) officially formed.

1933

- Hitler appointed chancellor (January).
- Reichstag building burns and Marinus van der Lubbe arrested for arson (February). Today, it is hard to determine who set the fire—the Communists or the Nazis—but it is agreed that Hitler used the event as a pretext to eliminate political opposition and to frighten the German people into casting their votes for the Nazi Party.
- Enabling Acts grant Hitler dictatorial powers (March).
- Nazis boycott Jewish stores and businesses (April).
- Nazis burn un-German books (May).
- The People's Radio is unveiled at the Tenth Radio Exhibition (August).

1934

- Van der Lubbe is executed for setting fire to the Reichstag (February).
- President Hindenburg dies and Hitler becomes Führer (August).

1935

- Hitler initiates mandatory Reich Labor Service for young people and begins to rearm Germany.
- Nazis pass the Nuremberg Race Laws against the Jews, stripping them of all political and civil rights. The Race Laws identified a Jew as anyone who had three or four Jewish grandparents (September).

1936

- The Gestapo are placed above the law (February).
- German troops reoccupy the Rhineland (March).
- Summer Olympic Games are held in Berlin (August).
- The Hitler Youth law makes membership compulsory for all eligible youth, ages 10–18 (December).

1938

- Germany annexes Austria (March) and the Sudetenland (November).
- Nazi-orchestrated riots against Jews (Kristallnacht) take place all over Germany, killing 236 Jews; burning 1,300 synagogues; vandalizing and destroying more than 7,000 Jewish shops, businesses, schools, and private homes; and arresting more than 30,000 Jews, many never to be seen again. Two days later,

the Nazis ordered the Jews to pay one billion Reichsmarks (about $400 million) as punishment for a Nazi official's death (November).

1939

- Hitler threatens Jews during speech to Reichstag.
- Germany annexes Czechoslovakia (March). Hitler toughens Hitler Youth law, conscripting remaining eligible youth (March). Hitler Youth membership now totals more than seven million boys and girls.
- Hitler and Stalin create the German-Soviet Nonaggression Pact (August).
- On August 31, the SS dress in Polish uniforms and launch a fake attack on a German radio station in southwest Poland. The next day, Adolf Hitler lies, claiming that Polish soldiers fired upon German soldiers, and he orders the invasion of Poland. England and France declare war on Germany (September).
- Poland falls (September).
- The Extraordinary Radio Law is passed, making the intentional listening to enemy propaganda an offense punishable by death (September).
- The first deportation of Jews to concentration camps in Poland (October).

1940

- British bombing raids begin over Hamburg.
- Nazis begin Battle of Britain bombing campaign (July).
- Germany conquers Denmark, Norway, France, Belgium, Luxembourg, and the Netherlands.

1941

- Rudolf Hess, the third highest-ranking Nazi, deserts and flies secretly to England to negotiate a peace agreement (May).
- Greece and Yugoslavia fall to Germans.
- Yugoslavia, Greece, Bulgaria, Italy, and Romania join Nazis.
- Germany invades Soviet Russia (June).
- German Jews must wear Jewish star (September).
- Mass murder of 33,000 Jews at Babi-Yar in Soviet Russia (September).
- Germany declares war on the U.S. (December).

1942

- Nazis hold Wannsee Conference to formalize plans for the "final solution of the Jewish problem" (January).

- German army lays siege to Moscow and heads toward Leningrad (October).

1943

- Germany suffers a major defeat at Stalingrad (January).
- Allies carpet bomb Hamburg, killing at least 43,000 (July).

1944

- Allied troops launch D-Day invasion (June).

1945

- Germany collapses as Allies invade (February–April).
- Hitler commits suicide in his bunker, but the Nazis lie, telling the German people that Hitler was killed at the head of his troops while defending Berlin (April).
- Germany surrenders unconditionally (May).

For more about the book, go to . . .

THE BOY WHO DARED
TEACHING GUIDE

www. scholastic.com/discussionguides

BIBLIOGRAPHY AND FURTHER READING

This book has been greatly informed by Karl-Heinz Schnibbe and Gerhard Kunkel, whom I was privileged to interview in their homes, through e-mail, and over the telephone. In the midst of writing this book, I learned that Gerhard passed away. He was eighty-five years old.

For those wishing to read a factual account of Helmuth's life and the lives of Rudi Wobbe and Karl-Heinz Schnibbe, I recommend Rudi Wobbe's memoir, *Before the Blood Tribunal*; Karl-Heinz Schnibbe's memoir, *The Price*; and Blair R. Holmes and Alan F. Keele's wonderfully sourced and documented *When Truth Was Treason: German Youth Against Hitler*. For those who read German, Ulrich Sander's *Jugendwiderstand im Krieg: Die Helmuth-Hübener Gruppe 1941/1942* provides an outstanding collection of primary source material and documents. Quotations on pages 125, 136–137, 144, 146, 158–159, 161, 162, 170–171, and 173–174 have been translated from Sander's book, and are used with permission from Pahl-Rügenstein Verlag (Bonn, Germany). I thank Brigitte Weinsteiger and Erika Weinsteiger for their translation.

Young readers interested in another fictional treatment of Helmuth's story will enjoy Michael Tunnel's *Brothers in Valor* (Holiday House, 2001).

For background research on life in Germany during the Third Reich, I am grateful to the following select sources: William L. Shirer, *The Rise and Fall of the Third Reich, Berlin Diaries*; H. W. Koch, *The Hitler Youth: Origins and Development*; David Crew (editor), *Nazism and German Society*; C. L. Sulzberger, *New History of World War II* (revised and edited by Stephen Ambrose); John Toland, *World War II*; Fritz Brennecke, *Nazi Primer: Official Handbook for Schooling the Hitler Youth* (translated by Harwood I. Childs).

For Hitler's words and the BBC broadcasts found on pages 21, 98, 109, and 114, I drew from Hitler's *Speeches and Proclamations 1932–1945: The Chronicle of a Dictatorship*; and contemporaneous articles published in *The New York Times* and the *Völkischer Beobachter*.

The official records of Helmuth Hübener's arrest and trial are archived in the Bundesarchiv (Berlin, Germany). I thank Herr Grunwald for his long-distance assistance in obtaining document groups NJ 1125, R 3017/8, J 127/42g, and RY 1/2/3, 147. Quotations on pages 140–141, 161, 162, and 169–170 are translated from these documents.

The worst experience can bring out a person's deepest strength. When some people are hit by adversity, they show an amazing capacity for survival, heroism, and faith. To better understand this strength, I read books such as Al Siebert's *The Survivor Personality* and Laurence Gonzales's *Deep Survival*. I also turned to the life and writings of the deeply spiritual theologian and Nazi-resister Dietrich Bonhoffer, who was executed by the Nazis in 1945. These writings included *Ethics, A Testament to Freedom: The Essential Writings of Dietrich Bonhoffer*, and most especially, *Letters and Papers from Prison*.

It surprises some people to learn that the Church of Jesus Christ of Latter-day Saints (LDS) has been in Germany since 1840. The church had about one thousand members living in Hamburg during the war.

I am grateful to the LDS church for honoring and preserving Helmuth's memory in the invaluable archives found in the Historical Department of the Church of Jesus Christ of Latter-day Saints in Salt Lake City, Utah. I thank LDS church members Nadine Hubbard (Moscow, Pennsylvania) and Tim Wadham (Phoenix, Arizona) for reading this manuscript and for answering my many questions. The LDS Web site (www.LDS.org) and Drew Williams's *A Complete Idiot's Guide to Understanding Mormonism* furthered my understanding of the Mormon faith.

I am also grateful for the work of Johannes Brahms, who was born in Hamburg. His masterpiece *Ein deutches Requiem*, or *German Requiem*, offers a sacred "mass for humanity" that emphasizes comfort for the living, and that inspired and sustained me during the writing of this book.